PRETTY THUGS 4

SA'ID SALAAM

URBAN AESOP PUBLICATIONS

Email: Saidmsalaam@gmail.com

Cover Designer: Adriane Hall

Proofreader: KaiCee White

PRETTY THUGS 4

Written and Directed
by
Sa'id Salaam

Visit prettythugs.net for exclusive Pretty Thugs
merchandise!

CHAPTER 1

"**D**rop the gun!" the hired gun shouted and shot. The bullet sailed right by his intended target and slammed into Young Vaughn's chest. The impact lifted him off of his feet and into the truck. Ironically he landed right between Zenobia's legs, which was where he was trying to go in the first place.

Lil Bruh spun with his gun and let it rip. He wasn't the best shot so he just closed his eyes and squeezed. The illegal switch in the gun allowed the pistol to fire fully automatic. One lucky round caught the security guard in his throat. The man dropped his gun as he dropped to the ground. He practically strangled himself trying to keep his blood from gushing from the hole in his neck. Lil Bruh remembered why he came and turned to finish the job.

Zenobia leaned up just as Lil Bruh raised the gun a second time. Life switched to slow motion mode, making seconds seem like minutes. She saw the malice and anger

1

etched in his face as his finger slowly squeezed around the trigger. All sounds went mute except for the harmless click of the empty gun. Life returned to full speed as he pulled the trigger again and again with the same results. *click, click, click.*

Lil Bruh had another clip in his car but not the time to retrieve it. He and Zenobia glared at each other for another moment before he turned and ran. She finally heard a gasp from below and looked down to the man between her legs.

"Vaughn! Oh baby no!" she wailed and rolled him over. Her eyes and hands scrambled to find the wound.

"Fuck!" Young Vaughn groaned and grimaced from the pain in his chest. Even with the bullet proof vest the slug still felt like getting kicked by a mule.

"Where you hit?" she asked as she continued to search for injuries and found he was still wearing the vest. Ethan wanted to protect his investment with the vest but also had a hefty Key Man life insurance policy on him as well. The bullet proof vest didn't just save his life, it also saved fifteen percent through GEICO.

"My chest! Fuck!" he grunted as people came rushing over.

"Z! Zenobia!" The remaining Pretty Thugs screamed as they rushed towards the crime scene. Everyone had ducked for cover when the shooting began, but popped up to take stock once it had ended.

"Vaughn!" Ethan shouted as he rushed to check on his investment. Especially since they needed one more shot to complete the shoot.

"We good shawty," he said even if he didn't feel too great. Ethan too checked for wounds in hopes they could finish the shoot since the shooting had stopped.

"Z!" Callie and Penny shouted over the chaos and shoved folks out of the path to their friend.

"We good," Zenobia seconded as her friends snatched her into a group hug.

The hired help didn't fare as well since he lost too much blood to maintain the grip on his neck wound. He blinked a few times before slipping off to his next stop. The sounds of police and ambulance sirens drew closer by the second. Which brought to mind the same questions they were coming to ask.

"Who shot you?" Ethan asked and leaned in for an answer.

"Ion know. Didn't see..." he said loud enough for Zenobia to hear. They made eye contact and came to a tacit understanding.

"Me either, just heard shots and ducked," she complied with the lie while wondering why. This was the second attempt on his life. Something had to give before he succeeded. There would be plenty of time to find out but first she had to repeat the lie a few more times for the police.

"Are you getting this?" Ethan asked the camera man. Rap seems to thrive on chaos and there was plenty here tonight.

"Sure am!" he happily responded. This was good footage for the shoot, the rest would go on his YouTube channel.

"T hank God!" Callie rejoiced when her eyes popped open the next morning. Something she usually did anyway but this morning was a particular reason to rejoice.

"Moving day!" Dominique cosigned from the other bed. The four bedroom apartment with three young chicks was a far cry from the luxury she had become accustomed to but it was better than the disrespect Mike was offering lately. She was used to an ensuite bathroom bigger than this hotel room but now had to wait for Callie to use it first.

"I doubt if them heifers are next door..." Callie was saying as she stepped into the bathroom. On cue a knock on the door made Dominique roll out of her bed.

"Ladies," she greeted as she pulled it open for Penny and Zenobia entered the room. Both were fully dressed and ready to go.

"Y'all must be finna stay here?" Zenobia fussed as she marched in. Some of that salt was from not being able to spend the night with Vaughn after the wild night.

"Girl, your hair is cute!" Dominique gushed and washed some of the salt out of her mouth.

"Thank you!" Zenobia sang while Penny just shook her head at the Jedi mind trick.

"At least they packed," Penny added since their bags were lined up next to the door. She tuned them out in favor of the happenings on her cell phone. Penny had become nearly obsessed with watching her followers grow by the day.

"Hey," Callie greeted as she traded spaces with Dominique in the bathroom. Her friends grunted in reply, without looking up from their screens. "Fine, thanks for asking..."

Dominique washed quickly, dressed and joined the rest. The events since coming to Atlanta had left her frazzled and scared of being left on her own. After giving Mike all of her, these girls were all she had left. The women dragged their bags down to their cars and checked out of the hotel. A short drive later they reached the Atlantic Station section of the city and moved into their new apartment.

"Girl!" Zenobia exclaimed as she opened the door to their new home. They had been here once before, prior to leasing but that was different. Now it was theirs, now it was home.

Callie let out a satisfied sigh only the previously homeless could relate to. Her friends had endured some hardships in life but none as hard as the shelters and foster homes of New York City. She looked up at the ceiling that represented the roof over her head and relaxed a little. Total relaxation could only come once she owned her own home.

"Right on time!" Penny cheered when she got a text from the delivery drivers below. Ethan had invested in his own future by buying furniture for the girls. Dominique refused the offer and went to blow up her air mattress. She was determined to get hers out the mud once again.

"For real, for real!" Zenobia cheered when a text alerted her to a special delivery of her own.

"Young Vaughn?" Callie guessed correctly and nodded her head.

"He finna help me put this stuff together," she said since

she had purchased a few items for her room that required assembly.

"Well, I'm about to make the runs," Dominique announced when she returned from blowing up her bed. Luckily she sprang for the upgrade that included an electric pump.

"Don't do nothing I wouldn't um..." Callie was joking until she remembered what she actually did with Savage. The brain is an amazing thing when it can literally tune out things the owner doesn't wait to own anymore.

"Save that chica! I'm about to go get my dick sucked!" she laughed even though dead serious. She had been sexually starved since coming to Atlanta since Mike was dicking down everyone else. Now she had a handsome, well endowed youngin who liked to eat pussy and had a little stamina. "I'm about to get laid!"

"Well, count the money first. Don't be tryna count with your legs trembling," Callie directed and she would know since Savage had her legs trembling as she drove home. "Anyway, here..."

"Word?" Dominique asked as she caught the keys to the storage unit. She had been there with all of the girls by now but still hadn't gotten a key, until now.

"Word cuz we heading to the studio later," Callie reminded.

"I'll be there as soon as I wrap up these runs," she said and rushed off.

"You gave her your key?" Penny asked when she realized no one was going with Dominique to the storage unit.

"Do you mind?" Callie asked hopefully, since she should have asked beforehand.

"Hell naw! Shit, she could have had my key!" she laughed.

"Key to what?" Zenobia asked as she came out. She nodded along with her friends in agreement when they filled her in. "Dominique is auntie! She a Pretty Thug too!"

"Come in," Savage called out in response to his doorbell. He looked down real quick to check his pose, then back up to see her face.

"Whoop, there it is!" Dominique laughed when she entered to see Savage reclined naked on the sofa with his dick laid on his stomach.

"Waiting on his new best friend," he said and made it move for her.

"He'll have to wait until we handle this business," she said and sat the bag on the table. The ten pounds inside made a nice thud when it touched.

"Right, right," he agreed and got up. She locked onto his butt cheeks as he bounded into the bedroom to collect the money. He was back in a flash with the cash.

"Bruh..." Dominique pouted when he stood over her while she counted. She didn't mind him watching, but the dangling dick was a bit of a distraction.

"My bad. When the wires coming off?" he asked and made her lose track when his dick wagged with the question.

Any man with a dick wants it sucked but her mouth was still wired shut.

"Never for that," she managed and started over. Once she got through the count she removed his bricks and placed the money inside the bag. "Now, where's your room?"

"Right this way..." he advised and led the way. She noticed him deliberately checking the time but thought nothing of it since guys do like to keep track of how long they stay in the guts. Kinda like they check the high score on the video game. She noticed but didn't care since she was just here for a nut. Or three which is why she saved him for last.

"Nice," she said of the king sized bed as she began to strip. She was really in the mood to have her boots knocked completely off so she stripped completely naked.

"OK then..." he concurred and kicked off his socks to match her skin for skin. Dominique laid back and spread her legs, then labia with her fingers. Savage slid between both, tongue first.

"Shit boy!" Dominique demanded when his tongue tickled her love button. She was in no mood to be teased so she grabbed him by the hook of his head and pulled him into her pussy.

Savage was the male equivalent of Super head. He drove his tongue inside of her while working his lips around her lips. When he added a little suction he kicked her off orgasm mountain and let her tumble to the bottom.

"Ready for this dick!" he asked, not expecting an answer. The dick was why she was here so he wrapped it in rubber and rubbed it in the slippery froth left from the nut she just busted.

Dominique thrusted her hips upward to get him inside of her. She wouldn't have to ask twice since he gladly plunged inside. Her legs went up to direct him to the bottom and he kindly complied. They grinded and groaned for a few cursory strokes before he got his feet set and gave her the business.

"Bout to, damn come again!" she fussed like it was a problem. It wasn't though so she grabbed his hips and nutted once more. Savage offered no reprieve though and kept on delivering the dick until another orgasm chased the last one away.

"Shit!" Savage warned when that good, gushy box started to get the best of him. He reached down and grabbed handfuls of ass so he could dig in and dig her out real good. Dominique had other plans though.

"Let me," she asked as no woman has ever had to ask twice.

Savage slipped from her slippery insides and snatched the condom off. He scooped a palm full of juice from her juicy box to use for lube. Not for long since a couple of pulls and one twist was all it took to make him explode on her stomach.

"Fuck!" he grunted, stroked and milked himself dry.

"That's right daddy," she purred and watched him skeet harmlessly on her tummy. Better there than taking a chance with the condom. "Get us a rag."

"K," he happily replied and missed her shaking her head at his bitch-ass-idy. Had he said, 'bitch you get a rag', he might have gained a girlfriend. He was back in a flash with a soapy washcloth, like a good woman does. He actually tried to wash her like a chick does a dick.

"Yeah, no, thanks. I got it," she said and took the washcloth to wash herself. He looked at the time but not for his high score. It must have been whatever time he was looking for since his doorbell began to sing its melodic song.

"Shit!" he fussed and scrambled to pull his panties on. They were actually boxer briefs but may as well have been panties as far as she was concerned. He was more woman than many women she knew.

"Then again..." Dominique laughed out loud at the thought of having a man she could control. Mike was definitely an alpha male and that turned out horribly.

She heard the muted voices in the front room as she got herself together. She let out a snicker since her legs were indeed shaking. Once she was fully dressed she grabbed the bag of money and went back up front.

"Thanks," Dominique was saying as she attempted to breeze through without meeting the man but it seems he was waiting to meet her.

"Hey there! We were just talking about you!" Robbie said from behind his Davinci persona.

"Me?" Dominique asked. She was so confused by the statement she actually turned to see if anyone had come out behind her No one did so she added a sharp, "Why?"

"Oh nah, cuz I was, well he was tryna get some weight, weight. More than I can stand," Savage explained.

"I have no idea what that means. Thanks for the dick

tho," Dominique said and blew him a kiss as she hit the door. There was an awkward silence since the undercover cop was here to meet his plug.

"Welp, I hope you can take dick as well as you give it. Cuz..." the cop threatened. It wasn't fair but some dudes tend to respond better when their bung hole is in danger.

"Wait! She's just the delivery girl! The other chicks really run the show!" Savage pleaded and squeezed his cheeks together tightly.

"Names!" he demanded.

"Even better..." the suspect announced and picked his phone off the table. A few swipes later he thrust the screen in the cops face.

"The Pretty Thugs huh?" Robbie laughed as he looked over the unlikely drug dealers. He was ready to make another rape reference until a familiar face tilted his head. He zeroed in on Zenobia and strained to recall, "Where do I know her from?"

CHAPTER 2

"I'm so nervous!" Callie admitted as she drove. She lifted one hand from the steering wheel and watched it tremble.

"For what? You got this! You dope!" her manager said from the passenger seat. Dominique had heard her practicing her raps while they shared the hotel room. Now it was time to lay them down on a track.

"Hope we got some dope ass beats!" she shot back and gripped the wheel even harder.

"The dopest! Adam Salah, MTuni Brown. I even got Sa'id Salaam to dig out an old track for y'all!" she informed proudly. A line up like that was guaranteed to go platinum if the Thugs brought some heat.

"P said Ethan got some beats too," Callie relayed. Two managers were already proving to be better than one. With them competing the girls would be the beneficiaries.

"Oh, OK. Yeah," Dominique added and nodded. The

moment was over when Young Vaughn's song featuring the crew came through the speakers. Both reached to turn it up and let it bang as they rode. The parking lot in front of the studio complex was full when they arrived. Both scanned the cars to see who was present. Penny's Benz was parked next to Ethan's Tesla since she arrived first.

"You good?" Callie asked when they both reached Mike's Maybach with their eyes.

"Yup!" she insisted through her wired jaws and hopped out before Callie could put the vehicle in park.

"Sup y'all!" Zenobia called out as she stepped from Young Vaughn's car.

"Ready to lay some tracks!" Callie cheered and led the way inside. All eyes turned to studio room A since that's where Mike and his team recorded. The door didn't open so they continued down the hall to room C.

"Here they go!" Penny announced when her Thugs joined her and the middle aged man in the room. He looked a decade younger with his trendy clothes and throwback Jordans. His knotty afro had a crisp line then ran into a tapered beard.

"Pretty Thugs in the house!" Zenobia proclaimed to the stranger.

"This is Malik, our engineer," Penny introduced as the man stood.

"Callie, Zenobia. Dominique," the women greeted as he made his way around with his hand.

"Few rules?" Malik announced but made it sound like a

question. The oxymoron had their full attention as designed so he went on. "I'm a non-smoker, so..."

"We don't smoke!" they all shot back in unison. Malik smiled, nodded and sat back behind the mixing board to get started.

"Can you pull up that first track Adam sent over?" Dominique asked as she took a seat behind him.

"Ethan wanted me to..." he was saying until he read the lines in her brow. "Adam Salah, coming up."

"Ooh, I like that!" Penny sang and stood when the melody began to play. Penny may have stood but it was P-money who began dancing. The bouncy bass line ordered her hips to move.

"That's the new P-money dance!" Callie declared as her friend shook her ass and swayed her hips.

"Let me get this!" Zenobia said and began to record.

"P-money! C-money!" Dominique chanted when Callie joined her. Zenobia handed off the phone and jumped into the mix. "Z moncy!"

"The Money dance!" Malik nodded and named the track. The girls picked up the chant and came up with a hook. "Get in there and let's lay that!"

The girls rushed into the sound booth and laid it down. Malik recorded everything including the laughter. A good engineer will record everything and piece it back together later. The same way Dominique recorded them throughout the day.

"What we got going on?" Ethan asked as he entered the

studio room. The smile and head nod said he liked whatever it was.

"The Money dance! First single!" Dominique cheered. She had a knack for picking singles and Lil Bruh's track shooting up the charts proved it. It was she who picked the perfect introduction to the world.

"Nice. We'll see about the first single," Ethan replied. He had two Thugs to her one which gave him some say in the matter. Plus he intended to outbid any offers and sign the group to his label. Penny blew a kiss from the booth and he waved in reply.

"Shoot," Dominique fussed when her phone buzzed in her purse. She had turned the hustle phones off so this was personal or personal business. Lil Bruh's name on the screen said it was the latter. "Hey Lil..."

"You fired!" he abruptly cut in and hung up. Dominique furrowed her brow in thought for a moment, then stood.

"Awe shit!" Callie said from the booth as she saw the woman storm from the room. Dominique marched down the hall and raised a hand to knock, before changing her mind and barging in.

"Fuck you mean, I'm fired!" she shouted down at him as she stood over him. "Nigga you must have forgot who got your ass off the block! You was selling crack and rapping to your boys on a corner until I put you on!"

"I, um, we, he..." Lil Bruh stammered and stuttered before looking at Mike. The same dude was just busting his gun trying to kill Young Vaughn but cowered when confronted by a woman.

"I can't understand what she is saying?" Mike laughed. The two young chicks flanking him laughed too even if they didn't understand any of it. He was mocking the jaw he had wired shut, they just laughed. Not knowing he would wire their mouths shut too if he felt like it.

"You gonna understand that contract he signed!" she growled through gritted teeth and spun on her heels. She would get her twenty percent through the courts if need be since the contract was binding. Mike was just doing it to fuck with her since he could no longer control her.

"Let me find out you're scared of a women," Mike snarled over at his rapper. He was already disgusted by the botched hit, even if the beef was boosting sales. Young Vaughn still had the star power his rapper lacked. Lil Bruh would always be second as long as Vaughn was breathing.

"You good?" Callie asked when Dominique finally made it back.

"Huh? Yeah girl. I had to take a walk and clear my mind," she explained part and the smell of weed on her explained the rest. "What I miss?"

"Only our first single!" Zenobia answered. They had matched up some of their pre-written raps and put together a song. The Money dance song even had a dance to go with it.

"You may be right," Ethan offered begrudgingly. He would have preferred one of the tracks he picked but had to admit the song was hot. Plus Penny loved it and he was starting to love her.

"Single? This shit is a movement!" Penny cheered and went into the dance when Malik let the song play.

"OK then!" Dominique nodded and smiled through her wires. She may have been MIA for a moment but quickly got on her job by recording a clip of the girls performing their dance while the song played. She instantly uploaded it to the Pretty Thugs IG account and had a hundred likes and shares before she could put the phone down.

They managed to record one more song before the end of their first studio session. The Pretty Thugs were on the way. Penny and Zenobia went to spend time with their men while Dominique had some runs to make. Callie thought she was going to get some rest but Brandon was blowing up her phone. She headed straight over to see what was so urgent.

"What the heck is so urgent?" Callie fussed as she barged in the room. Poor Brandon couldn't get the word out so he just turned his head. Callie followed with her eyes and found the problem sitting on his roommate's bed. "Alizae!"

"In the flesh!" the woman announced. "Have a seat we need to talk."

"About what?" Callie shrieked since she couldn't possibly know what they had to talk about.

"We'll be outside," Brandon said and pulled Rozz by her hand.

"Bring that sexy lil mufuckah back tho. We need to run a train on her fine ass!" Alizae called after them and cracked up. She enjoyed making people uncomfortable any chance she got.

"So what's up?" Callie barked. She wished she had her crew with her but wasn't going to show any fear. Not that it mattered since Alizae could smell it with her tongue like a snake.

"What's up is I'ma need some more bread," she laid out flatly. "Like, twenty racks this time."

"Fuck would I give you twenty dollars, let alone twenty bands for?" she reeled and winced like it was painful.

"Cuz ole boy getting out today. I dropped the charges," Alizae explained halfway. There was a lot more to it but none she cared to share. Snakes usually don't share well.

"And, how is that my business?" Callie reeled.

"Cuz, the people who stuck a gun in my mouth and made me drop them charges, wanna talk to you," she revealed. She took their money to drop the charges but wanted a little traveling money before she left to go back to New York.

"And again, how is that my business?" she repeated as the door opened.

"Oh hey!" Rufus cheered when he saw women in the room.

"Get out!" Callie snapped but got quickly overruled.

"Nah, stay!" Alizae barked and froze the kid in place.

"Whatever," Callie shrugged and turned for the door.

"Don't say I ain't try to put you on!" Alizae called after her. She shrugged too since she already took the money to give her up. Except she blamed a group of girls from Stone

Mountain who had jumped her over a baby daddy. Alizae turned to the nervous boy and barked again. "What's your name?"

"Um, R,r,Rufus!" he managed. "I'm Bran..."

"Let me see your dick!" she cut in and demanded.

"My,my, my..."

"Your dick nigga! Who you Johnny Gill nigga? Pull your dick out!" she snapped but didn't feel like waiting for him. She reached over and snatched him close by his belt. Rufus watched nervously as she unzipped his pants and pulled out his dick. "OK then! You one of them big dick nerdy niggas huh!"

"Huh?" he repeated since he didn't know he just happened to be larger than average. That didn't confuse him as much as the woman undressing on his bed. His dick sure understood and stretched out between them.

"You good nigga?" Alizae asked when the teen swooned and nearly fell. All the blood rushed from his brain to the throbbing dick in front of them.

"Yeah I just got lightheaded," he said and sat beside her.

"I got yo head young nigga," she laughed and snatched him by his neck.

"Mmph!" Rufus grunted when he found himself in between her legs with a mouthful of muff.

"Breath through yo nose!" she advised since she didn't want him to pass out. Not before she nutted in his mouth that is.

Alizae lifted her legs high and gripped Rufus by the back of his head. She pulled his mouth tight against her box and grinded. Grinded, Rocked and bucked against his mouth as he tried to stay alive. He messed around and tried to breath through his mouth and got a mouthful of salty pussy. Luckily for him and his family she got off fairly quickly, so he could breath.

"Take that nut hoe!" Alizae grunted and kicked her legs as she bust a nut. She had been hearing that since she was twelve so she gave it back any chance she got.

"Uhhh!" Rufus reeled and fell away when she released her death grip. He tried to look at her but his glasses were fogged up from the steam that escaped from that hot box.

"Un-uh. You ain't going nowhere!" Alizae laughed and grabbed him by his still erect erection. "Come on and get you some of this pussy!"

"You for real!" the nerd gushed and swooned again. Alizae pulled him back down by his dick and guided him inside.

"Now hunch nigga!" she ordered. Again, something no woman has ever had to say twice. The kid had one gear, fast. He took off at a hundred humps an hour. Luckily that's how Alizae liked it since her beat up box needed to be pounded. Alizae pulled her legs up and let him bungey off the bottom of her box. The door opened when Brandon and Rozz returned. Both were frozen in place for several seconds to process what they walked in on.

"No!" Brandon shouted in shock, while Rozz winced from the sharp smell of sex hanging in the air. It was too late though because Rufus let out a grunt and went stiff as he pumped her full of come. Brandon could only pull his girl away from the carnage.

"Damn nigga! You just bust in a bitch!" Alizae griped and pushed him out of her. Not that she really cared since she had a whole hustle dedicated to letting dudes nut in her. There wasn't enough time to run her pregnancy scam since her flight left in a couple hours. That doesn't mean she wouldn't try. "You just got me pregnant!"

"I did?" Rufus wondered in confusion. He had a genius level IQ but nothing is as confusing as that first piece of pussy.

"Hell yeah nigga! I need five hundred for an abortion! Unless you tryna be a daddy?" she dared.

"My mom will kill me!" he pouted. His lip began to tremble as a tear trickled down his cheek. "I only have fifty bucks."

"Come on with it," Alizae demanded and got dressed. It was less than she came for since she couldn't extort Callie out of more money. She did get a couple good orgasms out of the deal and fifty dollars to boot.

CHAPTER 3

In breaking news, star collegiate athlete arrested for rape has now been released after alleged victim recants story and refuses to cooperate...

"Dang! See, that's why people don't be telling cops nothing," Zenobia moaned as Icc appeared on the screen. He was giving a statement about clearing his name but the girls tuned him out.

"That's why you ain't say nothing about Lil Bruh shooting up the video shoot?" Dominique slid in.

"Facts! Cuz then I'm gonna be called a snitch and he just gonna get right out!" she shot back and fought not to get emotional. She knew better than most that snitches got stitches since she witnessed her brother get murdered.

"Word," Callie agreed. She could have easily gotten KT and Slime cased up for killing Voodoo since they were dumb enough to hold on to the murder weapon. Instead she took it to the streets and got real justice.

"He deserves whatever comes his way," Dominique gritted. She would still get her twenty percent off him dead or alive and she preferred dead after this. The room went mute in contemplation until the door burst open.

"Guess who out of jail!" Penny shouted when she stormed into the apartment.

"Ice. We know," Zenobia answered on behalf of her and Callie. "Ice just gave a whole press conference after the charges were dropped."

"They must have paid ole girl off to have her recant her story. Grimy bitch tried to hit me up for twenty bands before she left," Callie informed.

"Left where? Is she gone? Will she come back!" Penny and Zenobia peppered her with questions. They were on the verge of blowing up and didn't need anything coming back to haunt them.

"Don't know, hope so, better not!" she answered in order. Dominique didn't know the full story but did know enough about blackmailers to contribute her two cents to the pot.

"If you paid her once she'll definitely be back! People like that never go away," she informed. The room went quiet while they mentally chewed on that fact. Callie had more to chew on since she was the link between the two.

"Well, if she comes back she finna get dealt with," Zenobia declared. She may not have been a thug but her boyfriend was.

"Let's just hope she don't," Callie said. She didn't scare easily but Alizae was dangerous and she knew it.

"On another note..." Dominique announced to change the subject. She turned her tablet so everyone could see the screen.

"A million damn followers!" Zenobia exclaimed, while Callie added, "And a blue star!"

"I got one too!" Penny rejoiced when she saw her account had been verified as well. The other girls checked their personal accounts and realized they had blue stars as well. "Dang China, Turkey..."

"We need to get this album done!" Callie realized. The hype was well established. Now they needed a product to sell to the million followers.

"**E**than just hit," Penny said when there was a pause in their studio session. She quickly got up and headed for the door.

"Ethan about to hit," Callie snickered since her friend was officially addicted to dick.

"Mmhm," Zenobia agreed while she texted with Vaughn to secure some dick for the night herself.

"So just what is this big surprise you have for me?" Penny cooed seductively as she entered Ethan's office. She was actually a little juicy from the anticipation of sneaking out of the studio session for a quickie with her boyfriend.

"Someone I'd like you to meet," Ethan replied and nodded at the person on the sofa. "Doobie Daddie this is..."

"P-money!" the rap star cheered and rushed across the room to scoop her up. He picked her up and twirled her around while Ethan looked on.

"Hey Doobie," she greeted unsurely since this was quite uncomfortable.

"Wait, you guys have met?" he asked curiously, despite the obvious.

"Have we! Whew!" he gushed as she blushed, causing Ethan's face to flush.

"Oh, OK, I um," Ethan stammered as he searched for the train of thought that had been derailed. "Oh yeah! We want to feature you on a track with Doobie!"

"Yeah, Ethan let me hear y'all shit. You dope as fuck!" the rapper cheered. She was but she had an increasing following in places he wasn't. Being white and talented doubled her appeal. It was a win for both of them.

"For real! Hells yeah!" she bounced and clapped happily. "They're gonna freak out when I tell them this!"

"It's um, a duet," Ethan revealed as he cleared his throat. The single with Callie and Lil Bruh was eating up the charts so he wanted the same for his artist. The Pretty Thugs had next but he was playing the long game as well. P-money was a force all by herself.

"Oh? OK, I'll um..." she reeled at the revelation.

"Word. Holla at ya girls and see if they mind," Doobie said understandingly. He hugged her again before turning to the door. "Ethan got the track so you can write to it. Let me know when it's a go."

"Fa sho," Penny said as he and Ethan shook hands once more. They remained silent until he was gone and she spoke up. "Bruh said let him know when it's a go. Like, he just knows I'ma do it."

"You should do it," Ethan said rather clinically.

"You know what else..." Penny cooed as she came near and gripped his crotch through his Kakis. "I should do?"

"I'm good," he declined and spun away from the kiss headed towards his mouth. Penny had to pause to remember if any of the guys ever declined some head. None had, which begged one question.

"The fuck wrong with you?" she snapped.

"Just how do you know him?" he wanted to know.

"Know who?" she asked back since they were alone. Her mind caught up a second later. "Doobie? We met and hung out!"

"Had sex?" he asked.

"And grew my hymen back before losing my virginity to you?" she shot back.

"Gave him some head I presume," Ethan stated with an air of indignation that insulted Penny to her soul. She was too young and too naive to understand that men are sensitive creatures. With egos as fragile as glass when they're in love.

"Actually I did, while he was eating my pussy!" she hissed hotly.

"Well, ok. Don't let me interrupt your session," he said

and hopped on his laptop. Penny took the hint and stormed out of his office.

"What's wrong with you?" Zenobia asked when Penny returned pouting.

"Ethan a hoe!" she shot back, then regretted it. "He's just tripping."

"Over Doobie?" Callie asked since she saw the rapper pull away in a Lamborghini.

"Like he ain't fucked Jovita!" she confirmed.

"He did?" Zenobia and Callie both reeled in semi shock. Callie added a squinted, "I knew it! That's why she's so protective over him!"

"Why don't I grab a soda? Anybody want one?" Malik asked to give them a moment to gossip in peace. No one heard him as he left the room.

"That's how I know! She acts more like his woman than I do!" Penny fussed. Again, she was too green to understand that it was her fault for allowing it. She was young, naive and green so she shook her head and cleared the thoughts like an etch-a-sketch. "Anyway, Doobie wanna do a duet with me!"

"Do that shit!" Zenobia was the first to shout since Vaughn had just asked her to do one with him. They had even written it together but she wasn't sure how to broach the subject to her friends.

"Hell yeah!" Callie chased behind her. She almost felt guilty hearing herself and Lil Bruh on the radio every hour. Their song played almost as much as Young Vaughn featuring the whole group.

"It's done then!" Penny confirmed confidently. She

couldn't help but wonder if she and Ethan were too. She sent him a heart emoji on the spot but he didn't reply. She usually got back ten, today none.

"Hey!" Penny greeted happily when Ethan opened his door. She hadn't returned her calls or text so she decided it was best to just pop over.

"I wasn't expecting you?" he asked as she barged in on top of him.

"I see," she said when she registered the pretty, white woman seated on the sofa.

"Penny, this is..." Ethan began but Penny had left the building. This was P-money standing before them.

"Don't fucking matter!" P-money proclaimed and started to hop over the coffee table and snatch her blonde hair out by the roots. She quickly contained herself and decided to go a different route. "You can have him."

"Penny, wait!" Ethan called down the hall after her but she replied with a middle finger. He started to go down the hall after her but the elevator opened as soon as she pressed the call button. She ducked into the elevator and pressed the button for the lobby.

"Un-uh! Don't you dare!" P-money demanded to Penny whimpering in the mirrored walls. "No tears, no long ass post! Cheat back!"

"She's pretty!" the woman smiled when Ethan closed the door behind him. "Mom would love her!"

"Maybe, if she doesn't dump me for having my sister in town," he sighed. Ethan realized he had been wrong after speaking with his younger sister Arial. She was around Penny's age and era so he filled her in for her take on the situation.

"She'll be fine. Our generation swaps oral sex like chewing gum. She gave you her virginity. Not too many of them around," the younger woman explained.

"That's true," Ethan sighed. "I've never been in actual love before, so this is new to me."

"Call her." Arial suggested since she saw how upset she was. Emotions like that had led her into a mistake or two in her short life.

"I'll call her tomorrow," he sighed again and turned the movie back on. "Chewing gum huh?"

"**H**ello?" Doobie Daddie asked when he took the call on his business line.

He simplified his life by using different lines for different aspects of life. The family, his manager and close friends had the personal line. He kept another phone for his business interest and of course he kept a hoe phone, for his hoes. It was after usual business hours but since the number wasn't attached to a name he took the call.

"You busy?" Penny asked shyly and nearly hung up before he could answer.

"Nah, just answering random ass questions on my phone,

by unknown callers," he said and paused with her while she processed the sarcasm.

"P-money could never be random bruh!" she shot back. She couldn't see him sit up straight in his seat when he heard the name.

"Word," he agreed and reached for the blinker to change lanes along with his plans if she was trying to hang out.

"Are you busy?" she repeated and shook her head since it actually was a random ass question. "Anyway, my bars are done. When we hitting the studio?"

"It's whatever with me!" he shot back and changed plans. "My engineer is out of town but we can do it at my spot."

"Text the address. I'm on the way," she said and hung up. A split second later the address popped on her phone. She sent it to the GPS app and followed directions to his spot. By spot he meant condo in midtown.

"Yo!" Doobie said when she literally pulled in behind him.

He had just gotten off the phone making excuses for standing up his original date for the night. For one he was all about his music. The song would complete his latest project so he could go on tour. Plus, he wanted to see the girl again since they swung an episode a few months back.

"Yo yourself," she replied as she got out to follow him inside.

"Here," he offered and passed the thick, smoldering blunt as he unlocked the door. Penny paused and looked at it until P-money grabbed it and took a pull.

"Sheesh!" Penny exclaimed as they entered the million dollar apartment.

"Thanks. A lil something," he said cordially, assuming it was about the unit which was actually a lot of something.

"Welcome," she offered since she was actually referring to the warm glow of THC that spread through her body just from hitting the blunt twice.

"I'll show you the rest later. The studio is downstairs," he said and led the way. The finished basement boasted a bedroom, bathroom and fully equipped kitchen. Not to mention state of the art recording studio. Most of his albums were recorded right here.

"OK then..." she nodded and took another toke off the weed as they entered.

"OK then, pass that!" he laughed and plucked his weed from her fingers. Penny spent the time it took to boot up the system wondering what she was doing there. She had just about made up her mind to leave but got distracted.

"Huh?" she asked when the blunt appeared in front of her face. It was pretty self explanatory so she took it and took another toke. The strong weed mixed with the music and P-money began to spit her verse. Doobie was wide eyed with shock as she practically spit flames along with her rhymes. It was way harder than anything she had ever spit before. Then again she had never been this high before. A little venom dripped from the corner of her mouth as she spit ferociously

"Man, get yo fine ass in that booth!" he demanded and pointed. Penny smiled at the compliment he gave and the one he didn't. The order to get in the recording booth and the look on his face both said he loved her verse.

P-money put the headphones on and took position in front of one of the mics while he cued the beat up once again. He was recording when he joined her in the booth and took the other mic. The engineer would put the song together when he got on board so Doobie Daddie took flight. P-money growled and ad libbed into her mic and hyped him on.

He literally tore the track a new one but it was still breathing when he reached the end of his verse. Only for a second though because P-money went for the kill. Now it was his turn to hype her as she rode the beat like a dick. They free styled a hook and it fit perfectly. Doobie stepped out to run the track back so they could add the additional vocals to fill it out.

"Let's see what we got here..." he said and lit another blunt before starting the playback.

"Nuh uh! That's us!" Penny reeled when she heard the song. It was nowhere near done since the engineer still had his engineer thing to do. By the time he finished pushing slides and twisting knobs it would sound ten times better. Plus she was high.

"We got us a banger!" the rapper said, shaking his head.

"Un-uh," Penny declined when he passed the blunt but still took it.

"OK then," he laughed as she took a few more pulls off the weed. She closed her eyes and zoned out to the song that could take her from star to superstar. They didn't open again until the song came to a halt.

"Oh my God that's so dope!" she cheered and slammed into him for a hug.

"Shit, you dope!" he said as they held each other. They both pull their heads back to look at each other. They must have liked what they saw since they leaned back in for a kiss. It was just a smack but led to her shoving her tongue into his mouth.

They moved quickly before any second thoughts had a chance to take root. He took her by the hand and dragged her off to the downstairs bedroom. There was a race to the birthday suits that Penny barely won. Doobie did his Donald trump impression and grabbed her by the pussy as they resumed the kiss.

"Really?" he asked when she instantly soaked his fingers. That was cool but he hadn't seen anything yet. The real treat was when he slid a finger in that tight, little box. "Un-uh?"

"Un-huh," she giggled as they climbed on the bed. The kiss picked back up and he worked himself inside of her.

The rapper grunted and grimaced as he searched for a stroke. A stroke he never would find since she was too tight, too wet, and too pretty. Her whimpers and hisses only added to his problems. He was too high to solve the fast approaching dilemma. Too weak to pull out of the good, gushy pussy that was sucking him in. Too high to make an intelligent decision.

"Fuck it," he decided and bust inside of her. They made out like young lovers as he filled her full of tiny little

Doobies. Penny didn't reach her own orgasm but was still sexually satisfied.

"Mmmm," she moaned and rubbed his back as he gasped for breath. His breath and common sense both returned a few minutes later.

"Shit!" he fussed at himself over the raw sex. The last thing he needed on his rise to the top was unwanted children. One day he would meet his wife Taylor and their son Ramel would be no accident.

"I know right," Penny sighed woefully. Now that the pleasure began to wane, regret began to seep in. She thought cheating back would vindicate her but it didn't. "I'm going home."

"No you're not," Doobie said as he rolled out the bed. She had a 'huh?' on her face so he explained as he pulled his drawers back on. "You've been smoking gas. Can't let you drive like that shawty. Get some sleep."

Penny smiled softly at the love as he left the room. Cuddling would be too personal so he retreated up to his own bedroom and let her sleep until morning.

CHAPTER 4

"**G**et the door!" Penny shouted from under her shower. She could hear the doorbell ringing but no one could hear her.

"Someone get the door!" Zenobia yelled from her bed since she didn't feel like getting up. She had eased in just a few minutes before Penny did and got in bed.

"Tuh!" Callie huffed and pulled her comforter over her head.

"Why don't I get it," Dominique quipped and got up. She knew whoever was ringing wasn't coming for her but pulled the door open anyway. "Jovita?"

"Good morning Dominique," she greeted and stepped inside. "We set up a photoshoot for our clients."

"Oh, OK," Dominique agreed and nodded as she turned to get the girls. She was halfway through the turn when she fully processed the statement so she completed a 360 to face Jovita again. "Your clients as in, just Penny and Z?"

"Well they are the only ones signed to our management..." she informed smugly. Dominique pursed her lips to keep the curses from slipping out while she pondered a more tactful approach.

"You know one of the games Mike tried to play was divide and conquer. It didn't work. Only made the girls closer," she revealed. The smugness remained so she continued. "Why don't I pay whatever to include my client?"

"Make-up, wardrobe, hair, photographer, caterer?" Jovita rattled while she nodded to all of it. "Ten grand."

"One sec," Dominique said and spun once more. She marched down the hall and into her bedroom. Dominique was building a nice little nest egg from her cut of the drug sales. She had plans for the money but they just went out of the window. The ten grand was half of what she had but she also knew she couldn't compete with Ethan's deep pockets.

"What's up?" Callie asked as she stepped out of her room to investigate the loud marching.

"Photo shoot. Get the girls and get ready," she said and went to pay Jovita.

"Thanks. I'll have a receipt sent to your office..." Jovita smirked since she knew this was her office.

"What's going on?" Penny wandered out as if she had been there all night.

"Mmhm," Callie hummed sarcastically to let her know that she knew she just got in.

"Ethan set up a photoshoot," she replied.

"That's dope!" Zenobia cheered and bounced but Penny remained stoic.

"As long as he's not going to be there!" Penny fussed. She had decided last night with Doobie didn't happen so she was mad at Ethan all over again. Being mad at him sure beats being mad at herself.

"He probably won't since his sister is in town," Jovita replied and produced the address. "Don't be late!"

"They won't be!" Dominique assured and cracked her whip. "Let's move it!"

The crew complied and rushed to get dressed. They didn't have to worry about getting cute or doing hair since that was all included with the shoot.

"**E**than is the man!" Callie proclaimed when they arrived at the scenic loft that would serve as the set for the photoshoot. It's industrial charm and modern upgrades fit the rugged classiness of the Pretty Thugs.

"Psssh!" Penny blew her breath and the mention of his name. Still, she had to admit. "This is dope tho!"

"Word!" Zenobia cheered at the buffet line of foods.

"Mmhm," Dominique cheered when she saw the wardrobe stations set up. A few different clothing brands brought their latest designs, hoping to be picked for the video. The girls just saw free clothes but she saw an opportunity.

"Hey there!" the young lady sang happily when Dominique arrived at her racks of clothing. The competition to clothe the girls was fierce so she was delighted to get at least one. Until she realized this wasn't one. "You're not in the group?"

"No, I'm not. But if you would like your clothes on at least one Pretty Thug I suggest you get your boss on the line..." Dominique dictated. The woman complied and called her manager. The manager called her manager and the call was transferred again. Several sections later she found who she was looking for and struck a deal.

"Is everything OK?" the girl wondered when Callie returned her phone.

"OK, no. Dope, everything is dope!" she declared and marched away.

"Ooh! This!" Zenobia exclaimed and held a dress up to her body.

"This is me right here..." Callie was saying until Dominique came and pulled it away. "Hey!"

"Hey nothing chica!" she laughed and pulled her towards her new sponsor. "You just got paid ten racks to wear Iqra Ink clothing!"

"For real!" Callie shouted.

"Minus my fee, but yup. Plus a spokesperson deal in the works!" Dominique said loud enough for Jovita to hear. Jovita was no hater though and gave her a nod right before getting on her phone to work deals for her clients as well.

The girls selected their outfits for the various sets and sat down for hair and make up.

"Hello ladies!" Ethan announced as he walked in. Penny cracked a smile until she saw the girl from his sofa come in

40

behind him. Jovita came over and hugged her neck as he made the introductions.

"Guys this is my baby sister Arial. Arial, meet the Pretty Thugs!" he beamed, proving he was just as proud of them as he was his younger sister.

"Sister!" Penny shrieked as Arial came over. She made it a point to greet Penny first.

"Sorry we didn't get to speak last night," she greeted and hugged her.

"I um, naw see, we," she stammered and fought not to cry.

"It's cool. He told me all about it. I got him straight," she whispered. Penny flew out the chair and rushed over to hug her boyfriend.

"I'm so sorry!" she pouted as tears poured down her face and ruined her make-up.

"Whoa baby, it's OK! Not that big a deal," Ethan comforted and rubbed her freshly done hair. He had no idea those were tears of guilt since she slept with the rapper.

"I, but I, I," she stuttered, then clammed up. She had to come clean but this wasn't the time or place.

"It's OK baby. We'll talk later. After dinner?" he offered. Penny was still too broken up for words so she just nodded.

"You just destroyed your make-up!" Jovita said, shaking her head.

"Actually, it looks kinda cool!" Ariel said. "Goth even. Like Harley Quinn!"

"It does!" Ethan agreed and made a decision. He turned to the make-up artist and ordered. "Do them all like that!"

"Hells yeah!" Dominique agreed and cheesed as much as her wires would allow. She was glad they were coming out soon.

The make-up artist had fun making the girls look goth while the hairdresser mussed their hair to match. For the next few hours they assumed poses and snapped literally thousands of pictures. Dominique took some of her own to upload to the Pretty Thugs social media accounts. She tagged the clothing line and ad manager on Callie's personal page. The likes ran up and so did the bidding price to sign Callie as a spokesperson.

"Shoot, Brandon," Callie sighed when her play brother hit her line.

"Must be personal," Dominique guessed since she just dropped off and picked up yesterday.

"Better not be that broad!" she said through a snarl and stood.

"Want me to roll?" Dominique asked.

"Nah, I got this," Callie replied and headed out. Zenobia headed straight from the photoshoot to see Young Vaughn so he could see her make-up. That left Dominique and Penny since she wasn't meeting Ethan and Arial until later.

"What?" Dominique demanded when Penny came pouting by.

"What, what?" she answered with a question of her own.

"You've been moping since we got back. You and Ethan just made up which means some good, hot, make up sex, but you moping!" she laid out. Penny pouted a little more, blinked, then lost it.

"I didn't know that was his sister and he wouldn't take my call so I went over there and saw that girl on his sofa and thought that's why he ain't take my call and she was all smiling and I started to fight her but I just left instead and then I called Doobie and he was like lets hit the studio to do the song so we did and we did it then we did it then I find out that's his sister and they even look alike a little like their mouth and nose then says sorry and wants to take me to dinner and now I have to tell him!" Penny moaned in one, long, run on sentence.

"OK, you said..." Dominique began and took it from the top. She was able to break it down and put it together pretty well. She nodded along until she got to a certain point, then had to back up. "Wait, you fucked Doobie Daddie?"

"Yes!" she moaned and wailed some more. "Ethan's going to hate me now!"

"No he's not," Dominique assured her and wrapped her up. She held her tight and let her get it all out.

"You think, you think he will forgive me?" Penny asked once the sobs and heaves died down.

"Hell naw! That's why you're not going to tell him!" Dominique advised.

"But..."

"But hell! Men can't live with no shit like that. Girl, you

43

fucked up. It is what it is!" she cut in. "Now, you need to forgive yourself and take that shit to your grave!"

"OK, you're right," Penny agreed. She was right too because people make mistakes and the first step is to forgive themselves. "Shoot, he's gonna want some make up sex?"

"And he's gonna get some bomb ass head instead. Just because you made a mistake don't mean you can be a hoe. Put a little distance between them dicks!" Dominique said and patted her leg as she stood.

"You're like the cool ass, hood auntie I never had!" Penny laughed and stood with her. They shared a hug and officially became friends too.

"Speaking of head, these dang wires come out tomorrow!" she sighed happily. Dominique didn't have a man but did owe some head.

"Hey," Savage greeted almost shyly as he let Dominique inside.

"Hey ya-self!" she cheered and cheesed to show her new look. Like most men, he missed it so she pointed it out. "My wires are out!"

"Oh, ok. Cool," he replied stoically.

"Word?" she wondered since he kept on about her returning favor every time she bust a nut in his mouth. She had used her wires as an excuse but deep down knew she owed. Fair is fair plus she wanted to spite Mike even if he didn't know. Instead he got straight down to business.

"So, you got that?" he asked and looked down at the bag hanging from her shoulder. The money was neatly stacked on the table. She tilted her head for another angle of the deceit in his eyes and didn't like what she saw.

"Nah. Ain't shit going on right now," she said and she spun and raced for the door. It opened before she reached it so she spun and looked for another way. Cops came from the back just like the ones who came through the front door.

"Freeze!" a cop shouted as he snatched the bag away.

"That's not mine!" Dominique declared and would die on that. She twisted her lips when a familiar face came from the rear. Her head shook as she looked over at Savage looking down at the carpet. "Really?"

"Hands up," Robbie sighed and turned her against the wall.

"Ion know what's in that bag," Dominique repeated as he began to frisk her. He was pretty sure she wasn't armed but did want a chance to feel her up.

"Hold that thought," he said and started at her shoulders. Down her back, over her hips, then between her legs.

"You can get that," she promised when he cupped her crotch.

"I hear it's pretty good but, I'll have to pass on that," he chuckled and finished the search. He turned her around and pointed to the clock on the wall. "We watched you sell hundreds of pounds through that camera."

"That ain't all we watched!" Another agent laughed. The camera faced the sofa that hosted several of their sexual bouts. Which explained why Robbie passed on the bribe.

"She's got a mean backshot arch!" another agent grimaced and shook his head.

"Well, I'm sure you know the drill, but you have the right to remain silent..." Robbie began until the end of his spiel. Dominique just glared at Savage the whole time but he couldn't lift his head.

"Now, here's how this works," the second agent said and dangled his cuffs. That was Robbie's cue so he jumped right in.

"You can go to jail, or help yourself?" he said. If he was a betting man he would have lost all his money because he could tell she wasn't the type to tell.

"How?" she asked but it wasn't his turn.

"Well, we bought over a hundred pounds of weed off of you," the other chimed in and passed the invisible mic.

"Let's make it a thousand from whoever your supplier is," Robbie finished. "That means you can keep doing business. Keep making money, and stay out of jail!"

"Or, you guys can all fuck yourselves!" Dominique added another option and nodded in agreement with it. "Or fuck each other!"

"That's cool. Ole Bucky back-shot here tells us some girls are the plug," the second cop and came near to cuff her up. "Pretty Thugs for real!"

"I can believe it. Miss Zenobia Lowe got away once," Robbie nodded since he finally recalled who she was.

"Really Savage!" Dominique snapped and tried to go after him when he realized he gave up the girls. She was ready to do whatever time for her crime but the thought of her girls in trouble made her knees buckle.

"Whoa!" Robbie said and held her back. He saw the crack in her armor and tried to squeeze his way in. "Help them and help yourself!"

"OK," Dominique sighed and sat. "Them chicks were just delivery girls, just like me. I'll give up the plug."

CHAPTER 5

"We did it," Zenobia said in muted awe. It only took a couple of months but their album was finally done. It was better than done since each of the fifteen tracks could serve as a single. Each thug also had a solo song as a prelude to their solo careers

"We did," Penny agreed just as subdued. They may have been but Zenobia had a different take.

"Fuck yeah we did!" she cheered and jumped from her chair. "Play that shit back Malik!"

"Yeah, cuz I work for you," the engineer quipped but complied. The girls listened to the album they put together primarily with drug money. They were a hundred grand in but it sounded like millions banging through the speakers.

"Time to set up the listening party," Callie said to Dominique but would have to repeat herself since the woman was elsewhere. She did that a lot lately since she had so much on her mind.

"Oh, yeah! OK," Dominique agreed and began putting it in motion. She would rent a cozy venue to invite the heads of the several labels all vying to sign the viral sensation.

"Call that shit the duffle bag party!" P-money declared and got a high five from Zenobia.

"Facts! They gonna have to bring a bag if they wanna roll with the Pretty Thugs!" Zenobia added.

Penny had an inside track and knew Ethan was coming correct. She knew his offer would be in the millions, just not how many. He wasn't the only one since the girls were featured on the hottest songs in the country. The songs with Young Vaughn and Lil Bruh were still riding high on the charts but Doobie Daddie featuring P-money was the number one song in several cities nationwide.

Each label planned to bring a separate bag to sign which-ever Thug they could get to a solo deal. Penny and Callie had the most interest but no one would pass on Zenobia if they could land her. Her name alone guaranteed a platinum plaque.

"Can't forget this fuck man..." Dominique added devilishly as she sent an invite to Mike. Only because she knew he was too cheap to bring a big enough bag to land the prize. She just wanted to see his face when he got outbid and missed out on the hottest new group in the country.

"Word," Callie agreed. "Let's go celebrate!"

"I gotta make a run to Decatur to holla at dude," she advised and left off the name since Malik was present. He still had to mix and master the final product to present to the labels.

"For what? We finna be rich!" Zenobia cheered followed by Penny. Their mission was accomplished. They had plenty of cash so they were done with the drug game. "For real. Let's quit while we are ahead!"

"Plus the check from Iqra Ink coming soon!" Callie reminded since Dominique had secured a million dollar offer for Callie to represent their brand. Jovita had similar deals on the line for Penny and Zenobia. They were all contingent on their record deal. All deals allowed the flexibility for them to still push their own merchandise.

"Last one then," Dominique had to ask since it was their money she would flip. "Ion wanna leave Savage high and dry."

"Fuck him," Callie was the first to announce. Quickly seconded and thirded by her girls. "Pretty much. Fuck him."

"I might just do that one last time!" Dominique laughed but her mind was spinning a million miles a minute. She needed this one last flip to give the drug task force enough weight to set her free. Her mind came to a stop like the wheel on the Price Is Right when she came up with a solution.

"I can't believe you still hitting that!" Penny grimaced and shook her head.

"Cuz that hoe got some fiyah ass head!" Zenobia declared. She had Young Vaughn eating pussy now but he was no Savage.

"Yeah, I'ma head out," Malik said and shook his head all the way out the door. He had his fill of sex talk for the day.

"He can suck a dick!" Callie laughed. She would never

let it be known she slept with him too. Like Dominique said, some things have to go to the grave with you.

―――――――――――

"Hey there!" agent Robbie cheered when he opened the door for Dominique. She tilted her head and winced curiously at the warm greeting since they were anything but friends. "OK then!"

"Last time!" she dared and tilted her head to the other side.

"Absolutely!" he vowed and crossed his heart. This was a much better trade up than the hundred pounds they had on her. In fact, agents had followed her out to Decatur on more than one occasion. Enough to know Ant was selling a lot more than weed. They had more than enough to send him away for a lifetime.

"Well come on with that bread," she said since the government was fronting the buy money. All with the microscopic marks that would be used against him in a court of law.

"Guess you blew your re-up on the new Range?" he asked, mainly to let her know he was watching.

"Something like that," she shrugged. The government let them keep the proceeds of their sales so she copped a new whip.

"Well, be careful," he said with a touch of sincerity that made her furrow her brow. She was about to wonder why but he explained before she could. "Once this is over we should hang out?"

"So I can arch my back for you like in the video you like so much?" Dominique asked seductively and licked her lips.

"Actually, yes," he admitted and smiled.

"Where I come from it's fuck the police. We don't fuck the police!" she declined wickedly.

"I hear that," Robbie nodded graciously since he had a clap back ready. "I would tell you to fuck yourself but like you said, you don't fuck the police."

Dominique just blinked in the truth that she was the police too. Unlike Savage and most other snitches she wasn't snitching to save her own ass. No, she wouldn't let the girls go to jail. Not when they were on the verge of taking over the world. Especially when it was her who helped them get started in the business. When Mike chumped them off, she put them on.

"Call me," she said over her shoulder as she left the room. She knew her ass had an audience so she made sure to give him something to look at.

"**H**ey miss lady," a youngin greeted flirtatiously just like he did every time Dominique pulled up to the spot in the Eastwyck apartments in Decatur. Then, the other thing he did was ask, "Where is that white girl?"

"Hey . You know they in the studio!" she replied out of

habit. Penny had only come that one time but he always asked about her.

"Sup shawty. Y'all getting to it!" Ant said happily since he was getting rich off all the weight he was selling to Dominique. She had been coming back more and more lately and buying more and more weed.

"Yeah, you know," she sighed and twisted her lips. Dominique mentally mourned his freedom since she knew what was coming his way. It was him or her thugs so she placed the bag of marked money on the table.

"Say Lil Gip, brang her pack!" Ant called up the stairs. The order was quickly followed by the sound of footsteps coming down those same stairs.

"Hey Miss lady," the teen greeted when he arrived with the bag. "Sup with Young Vaughn?"

"He cooling," she replied and noticed the stars in his eyes. "I'ma see him later. I'll tell him you asked about him."

"For real?" he cheered but didn't wait for an answer. Instead he tore off to spread the word about their own hero from their own hood.

"A'ight," Dominique was saying as she stood until a commotion outside froze everyone inside.

"Twelve!" the teens outside screamed and cut out in every direction. Fitting since unmarked vehicles whipped in from each of those same directions. Regular police could have never made it this deep into the complex without the alarm being sent.

"Fuck!" Ant groaned when agents filed into the back way

he thought about running out of. He was down bad and saw no reason to make it worse so he raised his hands.

"On the floor! Hands! Get down!" agents shouted as red laser beams bounced around the room. Dominique looked genuinely confused because she was. Robbie gave no indication he was moving on the spot today. Especially with her still in there. Agents ignored the men and teens who ran as they secured the apartment.

"Clear! Clear! Clear!" rang from every room once it was cleared. The red beams stopped their eerie dance as the weapons came down. Ant, Dominique and another man lay face down with their hands secured behind their backs with plastic zip ties.

"Anthony Devoe. Marcus Grant and your name..." Robbie announced as he finally entered the unit. Dominique played along and understood why she was laid out as well. Now it appeared she had nothing to do with the bust.

"Pfff!" she huffed and rolled her eyes.

"Don't worry, there's plenty of time to get acquainted," he said down at her before nodding to his team. The men began to spread out and search the apartment. Not the gentle ruffle they did at Savage's condo. They had made it a good way up the food chain so they flipped the apartment inside out and upside down.

"Cocaine," one cop announced as he returned with a large bag of Columbia's finest powdered cocaine.

"Crack rocks!" the one in the kitchen called out.

"Got pills too!" yet another agent said and placed the bag of opioid pills with the growing pile of drugs on the table.

"What is this, Amsterdam?" Robbie joked. Only the cops found it funny but only because he was the boss.

"More like the OK Corral!" yet another agent said as he placed several guns on the table. The modified guns, silencers and scratched off serial numbers would add a couple more decades to their sentences.

"OK boys, take em away!" Robbie sighed like it was a chore.

"Separate cars!" his second in command added. "Don't give them time to get their stories together!"

"Up we go!" a cop said as he helped Ant to his feet. He escorted him away before Marcus was taken away next.

"You OK?" Robbie asked as he cut the zip tie and helped Dominique to the sofa.

"No!" she fussed and punched his arm. The aggression was just a prelude to the fear. "How do you know they weren't going to fight! All these dang guns!"

"That's why we came in the way we did!" he said and wrapped her up. He could feel her trembling in his arms and held her tighter. "I had to make it look like you had nothing to do with the bust."

"Can I go home? I just wanna go home," she pouted and pleaded. She thought she would feel relief once she saved her girls but didn't. All she felt was loss.

"Yeah but I'll take you in my car. An agent will follow in your car," he said. "Just put your hands behind your back while I walk you out. People are watching."

He was right too since a crowd had gathered to watch the bust. Some of the same teens who fled came to watch from a safe distance. There were many emotions on the many faces but Dominique only saw one. One face, one emotion as she locked eyes with the kid who served her.

"She's down with the lick!" Lil Gip declared and snarled at Dominique. She felt like he saw straight through her and could only duck her eyes. This chapter was finally over.

CHAPTER 6

"What do millionaires wear?" Callie asked the girl in the mirror. That chick had always been poor too and couldn't answer. They both just shrugged their shoulders and walked into the walk-in closet to find an outfit for the night. This was the night where rich men and a couple of women would throw their money at them for the chance to make money off of them.

A separate million dollar deal would activate the moment Callie signed on the dotted line. Penny had close to two million in deals lined up while Zenobia matched Callie's mil.

"You know what..." Callie told that chick in the mirror and approved the jeans and designer T-shirt she was already wearing. They did accentuate the fat ass in back and heavy breast up front. She didn't need to impress anyone since their music was already impressive. They had made it this far on pure hype, but their album was pure heat.

"Word!" Dominique declared when Callie came up front. She may have been dressed to slay in the tiny red dress and high heels but approved of her clients subdued beauty. The pretty, brown girl could have worn a burlap sack and still been stunning. She on the other hand had something to prove. Mike would be there and she wanted him to see how a real boss bitch gets down. Those kids he had taken a liking to couldn't do anything but make a man nut. She could make millions.

"Tadah!" Penny proclaimed when she came out and posed.

"Um..." Callie hummed and tried not to laugh. She looked great and made a dope appearance but there was one little problem.

"Awe man!" Penny groaned when she opened her eyes and noticed she had on the same outfit as Dominique. Different designers but little red dresses and heels none-theless.

"Twinning!" Dominique cheered. Penny pouted and turned to go change. "Wait! We're matching!"

"As if I want to match my auntie!" she huffed and stomped back into her room. She and Dominique had gotten much closer after their talk. She had confided something in her that Callie and Zenobia didn't even know. Something she would indeed take to her grave. At least that was the plan.

"OK then!" Callie applauded when Penny returned dressed rather casually. She rocked a tennis skirt, tennis shoes and polo shirt. Her hair had been in a bun but she took it down and pulled it into two ponytails.

"One more thing," Dominique said and came over. She sat Penny down and braided the ponytails for her.

"Someone needs to call Z-money and let her know we are dressing down," Callie said even though her phone was in her hand.

"If that heifer spent some time at home she would know!" Penny said since Zenobia had spent another night with Young Vaughn.

"Um..." Dominique hummed curiously since Penny spent half the week at Ethan's.

"Shoot, I need to get me some soon or my coochie is gonna close up!" Callie laughed.

"Shit, go get you some Pull-ups and spinna-night with Lil Bruh!" Penny cackled.

"I should," Callie laughed with her since she could have her way with him. Just wait until he drank and drugged himself into a coma and take that dick. The laughter came to a screeching halt when a familiar sight popped on the muted TV.

"Look! Turn that up!" Callie shouted and pointed at the scene on the TV.

'Drug enforcement agents raided a major narcotics supplier in the Eastwyck apartment complex. A large supply of drugs, cash and weapons were seized...'

"See! We got out just in time!" Callie told Dominique like 'I told you so', because she did tell her so.

"Bruh that could have been you!" Penny moaned to show what she thought of it.

"It wasn't tho. All that matters to me is you guys!" Dominique insisted and lifted her chin above the chaos she caused on the TV. "Come on now, let's go get this bread!"

"OK then auntie!" Penny proudly proclaimed when they arrived at the venue. They all rode over in Dominique's Range Rover for the big night.

Jovita often made slick comments on whether or not Dominique could produce but the woman proved her worth every time. Especially when the Pretty Thugs would have been in a jail cell if Savage had his way. Her biggest contribution and sacrifice may never be known if she had her way.

"Tell that board to quit trying me!" she shot back knowingly.

"Word, my manager is the shit!" Callie cosigned from the back seat. She looked around and spotted Young Vaughn pulling in and knew their third musketeer was on time.

"Ethan not here?" Penny asked since she didn't see his car.

The parking lot was packed with parties here for the listening party. Some execs had satchels of cash as signing bonuses. Some had some big ass checks, honorary to present for the prize. All had their spiels and terms spelled out in contracts. Some were written in stone since the CEOs planned to financially rape them with 360 deals, hidden fees and charges. Some points of some contracts were literally written in pencil since everything was negotiable.

"Yeah he is," Callie comforted when she saw his car pulling in.

"Fuck man here too," Dominique declared and nodded toward Mike's Maybach. She smoothed her dress to make sure he could clearly see what he would never get again.

Dominique indeed did her thing and the venue was decked out with Pretty Thug pictures and posters. A playlist from the album adorned each table to give a glimpse of what was to come.

"Look at this shit!" Mike said scornfully as he viewed the names of the songs on the album. Titles like Pretty Thuggin bothered him since he had a more ratchet image planned for the girls. Plus a million in cash to seal the deal. "Shit, how about Wet Ass Pussy!"

"Someone got that name already," one of his airhead arm pieces advised. The pretty little thing knew everything about every song and artist on the radio but no clue who the Vice President was. Mike would have had Kamala squatted down like Lil Kim too if he had his way. He hit her with the look and she muted herself like she had a remote control.

"Don't worry unc. The way I fucked Callie last time she definitely wanna be on the team!" Lil Bruh bragged. Only because he didn't know it was Callie who fucked him real good and not the other way around.

"And has she been back?" Mike dared and gave him the look too. He had a mute bottom himself and quickly hit it. They all watched as Jovita and Dominique took their clients around to meet the various movers and shakers. Some made preliminary pitches once they had an audience.

The crop thinned out since most only had six figure advances and 360 deals. Both agents let them know those were no-nos. So were any deals touching their merch since they planned to keep that lucrative source of income for themselves.

"So, Ethan ain't gave you no kinda hint as to how he's coming?" Zenobia asked and tilted her head at Jovita. Penny just laughed since she knew Ethan liked to announce when he was coming but that's not what her friend meant. She had no clue of how he intended to handle this business though.

"Sorry, nothing," Penny snickered and shrank.

"Actually, no! Which is weird?" she revealed. They had actually had several meetings on what terms to offer, how much advance, how many albums, solo deals. He finally just shut down and stopped talking about it. They glanced over and saw the Cheshire cat smile on his face as the masses looked worried.

Half of the suitors had been disqualified before the DJ cut the music so the show could begin. The Thugs gathered at their table while the DJ took the mic.

"OK people! Y'all know why we are gathered here today!" he began, then paused for applause. "Without further ado, I present to you..."

"Um, excuse me!" Ethan announced from a cordless mic at his table and stood.

"My nigga," Penny smiled proudly since he was clearly up to something. All eyes were on him so he began.

"I don't need to hear the album because honestly I have no intention of letting anyone sign this group besides me. I intend to beat any offer, sight unseen!" he said plainly.

"Sound, unheard," Penny correctly. It was cute but no one else laughed. "Excuse me..."

"I don't need to hear it either," Another exec announced and stood. "And I have a one hundred thousand dollar advance. Each!"

"Bwahaha!" Jovita laughed loudly. "These girls spent a hundred grand of their own money to produce their own album! And you want to loan them that much?"

"I have a two hundred and fifty thousand dollar advance, each!" another exec said and stood.

"For a ten album deal?" Dominique huffed and flipped her hair to show what she thought of that. A few more offers were made around the room but all got shot down. Finally Mike stood and walked over to Ethan. He snatched the mic from his hand to make his own pitch.

"Fuck all that! I got a million dollar advance, in cash. Right the fuck now for y'all to sign with me!" he said and bust a 'how you like me now' stance. "Oh yeah, and I'll throw y'all huned bands back. No recoup!"

All eyes went wide at the largest offer so far. Heads shook since no one planned on giving anything near that amount. Mike didn't even want the album since he had some raunchy lyrics and titles all planned out for the girls. Poor Lil Bruh wanted to cry since he hadn't received anywhere near that much money. Plus Mike's tricky accounting practices kept him practically broke.

"Like I said," Ethan said at the top of his lungs since Mike took his mic. "I have no intention of letting anyone sign this group besides myself. He was done talking to the masses so he turned directly to the Pretty Thugs. "I'm going to give you a million dollars, each. Bonus, no recoup. Sign with me."

"OK!" Penny sang and danced in her seat. The other girls like the other people in attendance just blinked to process what they just heard. Some sighed, stood and walked out since they couldn't fuck with the offer.

Dominique looked over to Mike and smiled as the veins in his neck all protruded. He was so mad he looked like he would explode. She recognized the woman who came over and whispered in his ear before he imploded. She was from the parent company and had deep pockets of her own. Whatever she whispered dosed the fire in his head and spread a smug look on his face. He lifted the mic and made a counter offer.

"I'll match the three mil, no recoup. And still pay the hundred you spent!" he dared.

"Submit your offers in writing for review and we will make a decision soon!" Callie decided on behalf of everyone. Both Jovita and Dominique looked confused but ultimately she was in control and they knew it. She stood to leave while Dominique went to collect their music from the DJ.

"What are you doing?" Penny asked through gritted teeth so no one could hear.

"Chill. We are going with your man. He may want to give us more money," she whispered back as they walked out.

Zenobia was behind them but not as close since she wasn't leaving Vaughn.

"Knew you were smart!" Dominique laughed as she caught up. The venue quickly emptied since no one else was matching that offer.

"Fuck ass white boy!" Mike glared at Ethan on his way out with a smirk, while Lil Bruh moped behind. "And you bet not cry! You need to man the fuck up! Matter fact, stay the fuck away from me until you can do something right!"

Ethan just glared back as Mike walked away. He wasn't afraid of him even though he really should be. He had no doubt he was whispering about him in the rapper's ear.

"What are we going to do? We can't even afford what you offered!" Jovita reeled once they were alone. She knew they didn't have that much cash in their coffers.

"I'm paying the bonus from my personal money. I'll get it back," Ethan shrugged calmly. He would make that back just from the management deal but he was confident in his stroke.

"Not if they sign with them! The stroke ain't all that!" she fussed since she knew about his stroke first hand.

"Callie just wants to see if I'll go up. I won't but she still won't sign with him. We're family!" he nodded.

CHAPTER 7

"So what y'all finna do?" Young Vaughn asked even though he had an answer for her. "sign with Ethan man. He cool a fuck and the bread right!"

"Definitely right," she agreed and went back to the most pressing thing on her agenda. She was still trying to figure out the best way to tell him what she had to tell him. He would be the first to know which would make it easy when she told her girls. That took precedence over whatever he was saying since she didn't hear a word of it. She almost forgot about him until he pulled into the parking lot of Sahirah's cookie shop. "Why you stopping?"

"So, you ain't heard nothing I just said huh?" Vaughn asked and twisted his lips.

"Yeah! You said you finna get me some cookies!" she guessed since they were at the cookie shop.

"Mmhm," he hummed and leaned over to kiss her cheek. "I'll be right back."

"We'll be right here," she said to his back as he entered the store. She liked being part of a plural and cracked a smile. She pulled the positive pregnancy test from her purse and sat it on his seat. She shook her head when she changed her mind and picked it back up. She went back and forth on the best way to tell her she was pregnant.

She hadn't figured it out by the time he paid for his snack and turned back for the door. He was happily munching his cookie when time suddenly slowed to a crawl. Zenobia watched as Vaughn's eyes went wide with shock tinged with fear. Two men ran up in slow motion and raised the mean little weapons known as Draycos. The AK/47 machine pistols ripped and sent the large 7.62 slugs speeding towards him. He reached for the ubiquitous pistol he toted to put up a fight.

Time resumed normal speed as the rounds found their target. Vaughn did a shimmy as they tore through his torso. His arms flailed but he did manage to squeeze one shot off. There is no such thing as luck so the lucky shot was pre-decreed to find its way through his killer's ski mask and out the back of his head.

Time slowed again as the last man standing turned the gun on the car they had been following for miles. Zenobia was frozen and couldn't duck when the tip of the gun exploded in violence once again. She sighed and accepted her fate but her story wasn't written to end here.

It took a few reverberated rounds before the shooter remembered the car was bulletproofed. Which was why they waited for him to make a stop in the first place. Vaughn's sweet tooth most likely saved Zenobia's life since they would have gunned her down as well if they made it to the store they were heading to.

"Oh no! No!" Callie pleaded when they arrived at the crowded crime scene. News of the shooting traveled at the speed of social media and the girls came running.

"Oh man! That's him!" Penny wailed when she saw Young Vaughn laid out in front of the store. There were plenty of police and paramedics milling about but no one was checking on him. Which meant he was already gone.

"I bet that's that damn Lil Bruh in that ski mask!" Dominique growled at the body laid out near the car. Luckily for him he was dead too because she might have killed him on the spot.

"Where the fuck is Z!" Callie shouted when she didn't see her anywhere. Then she spotted her still sitting in the front seat, staring straight ahead. They ran through the crowd towards the car and tried to dip under the crime scene tape. That almost caused a second crime scene when cops tried to stop them.

"Whoa! Crime scene!" he announced as if they couldn't tell that on their own.

"What's going on?" the detective demanded as he went to investigate.

"Sarge, these girls say they're her sisters?" a beat cop told the homicide detective since they couldn't get Zenobia to open the door. She was in a complete state of shock and hadn't budged since the shooting stopped. The bulletproof car was reinforced which meant no one was getting in unless she opened the door.

"You guys know her?" the detective asked as part of his detecting. He tilted his head at the white girl like he didn't detect her being her sister.

"Didn't he just tell you we did!" Dominique snapped.

"Let em pass," the man sighed and stepped aside. He damn sure couldn't get the girl inside to budge so maybe they could.

"Zenobia! Z! It's us!" they all called while waving and tapping on the window. Zenobia was gone into another realm and didn't even hear them. She stared straight ahead and didn't blink.

"Fuck this," Callie grunted when nothing worked. She climbed on the hood of the car and got right in her face. "Z!"

"Callie?" Zenobia asked when she registered her friend. Now she really was confused as to how her friend got where she was.

"Yeah girl. It's me. I need your help!" she asked. "Open the door."

"OK," Zenobia finally agreed and opened the door. She had been completely stuck but hearing her friend ask for help quickly unstuck her.

"She's in shock!" a paramedic declared as he rushed forward and plunged a syringe into her arm.

"What the fuck was that!" Penny demanded hotly. The last thing her friend needed was drugs in her system to heal her mental state. That's how people fuck themselves up by turning to chemicals to heal emotions.

"Something to help her rest," he said as they escorted her to the waiting ambulance.

"I'm going!" Callie insisted and climbed on board.

"Me too!" Penny said and followed her as well. The paramedics began to complain but the detective shut them down. The girl held up the investigation for an hour when she was stuck in the car. Her friends could get through when no one else could.

"I'll meet you guys there!" Dominique said since there wasn't any more room in the back of the ambulance. She turned to head back to the vehicle until she saw Lil Bruh laid out with the machine pistol in his hand. He was dead as a doorknob under the ski mask but she still had to give him a kick. "Bitch ass nigga! Good for you!"

"Uh, someone wanna get her?" the detective asked as she played kickball with the dead head.

"Whoa!" a cop said as he pulled her away. He held her back while the medical examiner came over. He used his pen to lift the mask up but to Dominique's surprise it wasn't who she expected.

"Do you know him?" the detective asked when he detected she did by the look on her face.

"Huh? Yeah, I mean no!" she said as she looked down at Lil Gip. If he was the killer that meant Vaughn got killed over the raid. Which in turn meant she got him killed.

"**E**than!" Jovita called out when her boss had drifted away once again. He didn't do social media so it was the call from Penny at hospital that relayed the bad news.

"Yes?" he asked as he came back to the same grim reality she just shared. Luckily those paramedics weren't around or they would have shot him up too.

"I'm sorry boss. He's gone," she repeated since she had gone the extra length to confirm the reports floating around the internet. She had called Dominique and got first hand reports of the facts before coming to relay the bad news.

"I um, he, we um?" Ethan stammered in his confusion. He had hired security to keep the man safe but they failed. In fact they drove off once the shooting started. "We need to, um?"

"We need to sign the Pretty Thugs," she reminded. She hated to talk business at a time like this but without the Pretty Thugs there was no business. The key man policy they kept on Young Vaughn would take months to pay out.

"Yeah, I um," he sighed and shook it off. "Yeah, I'll head over to the hospital now. Get them to sign the contracts. Monday I'll transfer money from my personal account to cover the signing bonuses."

"I'll dump everything we have into the promotion!" Jovita said as they headed to the door. It would take the million in the business account to launch the album as it should be launched.

They talked strategy all the way down the hall and into

the elevator. Jovita worked her phone to put everything they spoke of in motion while they descended to the parking level. They needed a video to promote the lead single, The Money Dance.

"Mash the gas on those spokesperson deals for P-money and Zenobia. That'll help with branding!" Ethan reminded.

"Will help with wardrobe cost too!" she replied. They were parked in different directions so the conversation grew louder as they grew apart.

"Don't worry, everything is going to be fine!" he assured her before turning to face the gunman coming towards him.

"Ethan!" Jovita shouted when she saw the figure pop up from behind Ethan's car. Ethan saw him before she did but it was too late. He was too close to try and run away so he charged forward.

"Argh!" Ethan growled as he rushed forward. He had won state in wrestling back in high school and planned to fold him up like a pretzel. The gunman's eyes went wide since he was used to people running away, not towards his gun.

'brrrr' the fully automatic pistol burped and spit six rounds ripping through his torso.

"Get the fuck off me dude!" the shooter fussed when Ethan got a grip on him. They wrestled over the weapon causing it to discharge once again. The rest of the extended clip emptied in a second. The slippery blood both weakened Ethan and caused him to lose his grip on his shooter. He had just slipped free when Jovita made it over to help out.

"Hey," she called out, causing the gunman to look her

way. They both recognized each other just before she pulled the trigger of her own gun. Ethan was blinking and gasping as she tucked her licensed pistol back into her purse. She then opened his back seat to drag him inside. "I got you boss! Just hold tight!"

"I'm holding," he whispered as she hopped in the driver's seat and pulled off. Lil Bruh felt like a speed bump when she backed out over him, and again when she pulled forward and raced towards Grady hospital.

———

"Why is she smiling?" Callie asked, confused by the mirth on Zenobia's face as she laid in the hospital bed.

"Cuz she high as a fucking kite!" Dominique fussed. She was completely pissed that the paramedics sedated the girl at all.

"Definitely high," Penny agreed since she popped a pill or two in her lifetime. Especially after the death of her mother. Her father helped get her through that pain but now he was gone too. A text came in and screwed her face even more.

"What" Callie asked.

"Jovita. Says she's on her way here? Ethan was hurt." she said over her shoulder as she rushed from the room.

"What now?" Dominique sighed as Callie rushed out behind her. She quelled her curiosity and stayed behind with Zenobia. The sudden movement when there had been none stirred the girl.

"Welp," Zenobia sighed and twisted her lips as she got out of bed.

"What are you doing! Where you think you going!" Dominique fussed.

"Going home," she answered both questions at the same time. Zenobia was unfortunately used to death since she had seen it so many times before in her short life.

"Let's see what the doctor says!" she said and went to find one. Meanwhile, Penny and Callie arrived at the emergency entrance just as Jovita rushed in.

"Please! He's been shot!" she shouted and sent the workers scrambling. There was a sense of urgency as nurses and aides rushed to her car parked in front of the door. They lost that urgency after looking for the man's pulse and not finding one.

"Nuh-uh!" Penny moaned when the nurses came moping back in to tend to the living. A gurney was wheeled out to collect the corpse.

"No P!" Callie pleaded when she went to the door. She tried to stop her but Penny pulled away and went to Ethan's car. He looked the same in death as he looked in sleep, minus the blood stained shirt.

"Awe man," she moaned once more and climbed into the back seat to cuddle with the corpse.

"What the fuck happened!" Callie barked in Jovita's face.

"Lil Bruh. He ambushed him in the parking garage," she said and slid down into a chair.

"He's not getting away with this! Not this time!" she barked again and went to help the staff with Penny.

"No, he's not," Jovita agreed. She would know since she knocked his life out a hole in the back of his head.

CHAPTER 8

Jovita joined the Thugs and Dominique for a mutual mope session after hours down at the homicide division. Of all the losses they took, this one hurt the most because they were right on the verge of blowing up. Only to have everything blow up in their faces.

"That's the last of that one," Dominique sighed as she emptied the bottle of wine into her glass.

"Awe man!" Callie moaned and started crying again.

"There's more where that came from," Jovita slurred and wobbled as she stood. She had every intention of drowning her sorrows when she came over so she brought several bottles.

"Ohh!" Dominique announced and rushed to the back. She returned a minute later swinging an ounce of weed in a zip lock bag.

"Hells yeah!" Penny agreed since she wasn't quite numb

enough. She grabbed the paper and a bud to roll up a fat joint. Obviously she was going solo since she asked, "Y'all not smoking?"

"Not with you I guess," Jovita laughed and rolled her own as well. Dominique followed as well but Zenobia leaned over snoring loudly. The combination of the sedatives from earlier and one glass of wine put her down like the opponent of a Mike Tyson fight.

"We chose him, you know," Callie said to Jovita as smoke filled the room. "Ethan. We chose him."

"We still choose him! Still the best deal on the table!" Dominique added.

"What?" Penny asked when she saw Jovita's face change. It was probably too soon to talk business but it was already in the air.

"The advance he offered was from his personal money, not the company," she informed. Even with the healthy startup cash they had yet to recoup from Young Vaughn's album just yet. Penny knew exactly what that meant and matched her sour face.

"So, we can still do it right?" Callie asked, looking back and forth between the two.

"His personal money will be included in his estate. Arial is his only heir, not sure what she will do?" Jovita explained.

"Well, we can still sign with the company. Fuck the advance!" Callie barked.

"Mike offered you a lot of cash," Jovita recalled. "You can take it or wait until the money comes in. You'll get the bonus he offered. I promise!"

"Fuck him and his cash! He did this shit! He put Lil Bruh up to it!" Dominique growled.

"Chill chica," Callie comforted. Only because she took comfort in the get back. Mike was going to pay for this one day. But he was going to watch the Pretty Thugs blast off in the meantime.

"I never killed anyone before," Jovita mentioned neutrally. "I mean, my dad bought me the gun because this is a violent city. I just never thought I would actually have to use it."

"Well he got what he had coming! Don't feel bad about it!" Dominique shot back across the room.

"Oh, I don't feel bad about it at all!" she laughed. "I wish I could do it again!"

"Well, once Mike finds out we signed with y'all you might just get your chance!" Callie nodded. The conversation tapered down as the women got higher and drunker. Penny tilted over on the love seat and went to sleep. Jovita stretched out on the chaise after Dominique and Callie staggered to their respective bedrooms. It was a long, violent day so sleep came easy.

Tomorrow would be another rough day since Ethan's sister was flying in to bury her big brother.

"I'm so sorry!" Jovita moaned and started crying all over again when she met Arial at the airport.

"I am too! Not surprised, but sorry!" she huffed. It was

clear that her anger superseded her sorrow at the moment. The bloodshot eyes showed she vacillated between the emotions all the way from California.

"Not...?" Jovita tried to ask but was pretty sure she didn't want to hear the answer.

"Not surprised! Not at all! I warned him about getting involved with these people!" she spat.

"Look Arial, I know you're grieving. We all are but, these people? What people?" Jovita huffed in indignation.

"Oh my God no! Not black people! Jovita!" Arial screeched, turning beet red from embarrassment. "Music people! That's what people! White, black, brown music people are all equally evil!"

"Oh, yeah..." she had to agree. Jovita always dreamed of becoming an entertainment lawyer and dealing with the biggest stars. She bypassed the Bar exam when she got on with Ethan and his upstart record label. Everyone she had come across besides him had been pure evil. Except the young girls with the troubled past and bright future.

"Now I have to bury my brother," she sighed as they made their way out of the airport. This wasn't a good time but later would be only worse once she got to see her brother. Jovita inhaled, exhaled and got to the point.

"I want to keep the company rolling. We are on track to make a difference," she said. "We will be in the black in no time."

"That's great. You should," Arial agreed.

"That's good to hear because Ethan made a commitment

to use some of his personal money to sign Penny's group. These girls are already stars! There was a whole bidding war and..."

"And I'm not giving you anything from the estate. I'm his only heir. I want nothing to do with or from the record label," Arial stated clearly. "You can have it all, but I'm not honoring any deal he made before getting killed."

"I understand," Jovita nodded.

"Oh, the police told me about what you did," Ariel said and stopped in her tracks to look Jovita in her eyes. "You know, with the shooter. Thanks."

"It was my pleasure," Jovita admitted. Shooting Lil Bruh in his face replayed in her mind every few minutes. Each time brought a smile to her face. They shared the moment then got moving again to go bury Ethan.

"I on understand how they bury people the next dang day?" Zenobia asked as the girls prepared for Ethan's funeral. Young Vaughn's people hadn't even signed for his body yet but Ethan was all ready to go in the ground.

"For real cuz black folk be sitting in the living room for two weeks before they get buried," Callie answered. It was only a slight exaggeration since it took just over a week to bury Voodoo. Mainly because his ratchet mother was too busy smoking blunts and guzzling malt liquor.

"He's Jewish," Penny replied, then sighed at her present

tense. Ethan was now in the past tense and that hurt like hell. "Well, he was."

"I know baby girl," Zenobia whined and joined her sobs. Callie felt her heartbreak since she knew the exact pain and angst they were experiencing.

At least she had the pleasure of the get back but Ethan already got justice. They still couldn't understand why Lil Gip would kill his mentor any more than people knew why Straight Drop killed Young Dolph. The late, great Notorious BIG said it best, 'it's the ones that smoke blunts witcha'. See ya picture then they grab they gats and come and get you'.

"I'm so sorry girls!" Dominique moaned and joined the group hug. As far as she was concerned justice didn't end with Lil Bruh laying in the same morgue. Mike did this shit as far as she was concerned and he was going to get his too.

"We're going to be late," Callie gently reminded. Penny bucked up, sniffled snot and stood to head out.

The girls loaded into Dominique's Range Rover and headed over to the Atlanta synagogue. Ethan and Arial didn't have any other family but their family was well known and loved. The proof was the packed parking lot full of mourners.

They didn't understand anything the Rabbi said but the service moved along rather quickly. It wasn't long until he was in the ground and covered with dirt. The sight was more than Penny could bear. She doubled over and lost her lunch right there at his grave.

"He loved you, you know," Arial offered and held Penny's

hair so she wouldn't vomit in it. "I don't know that he ever loved anyone before you."

Jovita rolled her eyes but held her tongue. Ethan wanted more from her than she could give so they decided to keep it strictly business. She too knew he loved the wild child very much.

"I'm finna go by the house," Zenobia said and sighed. The invite was open but no one took her up on it. Penny was queasy again and Callie was plotting. Dominique felt too guilty to go with her since she took the blame for the death. Instead, she had some plotting and planning to do.

Zenobia shrugged and headed out on her own. Her lips twisted at the old beater she still drove. It was fine just a year ago but she had gotten spoiled riding in expensive cars lately. She looked at Penny's Benz and Callie's newer Benz. Even Dominique was pushing a Range. She decided then a new car would be her first purchase.

She arrived sooner than she expected since she had zoned out along the way. It was pure muscle memory that guided her since her mind was everywhere besides behind the wheel. The women milling about in front of the house snapped her back to her grim reality.

"Um, can I help you?" Zenobia demanded hotly. She secretly hoped for some fuck shit so she could fuck someone up. She wanted to hurt someone to heal her own hurt. They looked like church ladies but she wasn't in the mood to hear chapter nothing, verse anything.

"Can we help you!" one woman asked in a demeanor Zenobia recognized. She had never met Young Vaughn's mother but she shared too many mannerisms and facial features to be anyone but.

"That's the girlfriend! I saw her on his thing!" the other woman pointed and bounced.

"I'm Zenobia. His girlfriend," she introduced but kept her guard up.

"Flora, I'm his mama!" she said with an air of authority like she was pulling rank. Even though a man's woman and mama hold different ranks in his life. Vaughn wasn't here to draw that line so they both held their ground.

"I'm Nadia, his auntie. I love y'all songs!" the aunt said and broke into a rendition of their song that embarrassed her sister.

"I'm here to collect his property," Flora demanded defensively. Zenobia's head tilted curiously since the two women were just looking around outside when she pulled up. The same head nodded a moment later when she figured it out.

"Ah, but you don't have a key," she declared and nodded with her assessment.

"And you do?" his mother dared.

"Of course. I was here every day. Got toothbrushes, clothes, shoes, panties..." Zenobia explained.

"We don't want none of your stuff," Nadia offered softly.

Zenobia went inside of her own head to process what was going on. She was here to collect her belongings as well as spend some time in the place they shared. Here to feel his presence, inhale his scent. Vaughn had a penchant for Killa cologne but made it his own since he smoked so much weed.

Vaughn's mother and aunt furrowed their brows at the faraway look in Zenobia's eyes and soft smile on her face. Flora softened when she realized how much this girl loved her son. She still wanted his shit before someone else got it. The mother and son had been estranged since he chose the streets over her sweet Jesus.

"Come on," Zenobia decided and hopped up the steps to open the front door.

"Girl!" Nadia exclaimed when she stepped inside behind her sister.

"Needs a good cleaning," his mother huffed at the ashtray full of blunt clips, game controllers and game accessories laying about.

"Yeah," Zenobia thought to herself as she headed into his bedroom. A glance back caught Nadia collecting weed clips and buds to tuck in her purse. Her head shook again as she continued on to collect her personal property. Vaughn was gone so his stuff didn't matter. It was just stuff so they could have it. She was given the chains and jewels from his corpse down at the hospital and would keep them. They could keep this stuff.

She gathered her toothbrushes, clothes, shoes and panties into a bag. One last glance around would have to serve as goodbye. Her eyes caught his most prized possession and most valuable. His mother and aunt were on a treasure hunt but she grabbed the real treasure chest. The notebooks full of rhymes and songs.

Besides, she had bigger fish to fry and a bigger decision to make. She was willing to trade her budding career to be his baby mama. Her friends would love it or hate it but it was her choice. Now that he was gone she had another choice to make. She grew up without a daddy after her daddy went to prison and knew what that life was about. Would she do that to a child was the question.

CHAPTER 9

Z enobia zoned out while driving. The radio was playing but seemed too far away to make out the words. If not for the turn by turn directions of the GPS she could have ended up in Louisiana. Thinking was dangerous so she found a spot and parked, before going to the entrance.

"Name?" the security guard asked when she reached him. He hated his job so he rarely looked up into the faces of the patrons. Sometimes he did since it was his job, but never in the eyes. The pain or indifference in the eyes occasionally kept him up at night.

"Um, Zenobia Lowe," she said and looked for her name on his clipboard along with him. They both found it at the same time so he pressed the button that buzzed the lock and allowed entry.

All heads lifted and turned towards the door when it opened. The prying eyes made her want to turn around but this had to be done. Her name was also at the reception desk where she given a number and took a seat.

Zenobia neglected her phone in favor of the number in her hand. Her mind reflected on other occasions in her life when she was given a number to wait for something. The nail salon, the welfare office with granny, and the deli section of her local Piggly Wiggly. It seemed so incongruent to this situation.

The door opened again and Zenobia's head lifted with all the others. The women in the room represented various demographics but shared a common goal, yet for different reasons. They all looked but the salvation they sought didn't walk in so they went back to their screens, pages or spots on the floor. Zenobia's head began to drop until she registered the face that walked in. It's owner turned to each side until they locked eyes. Both blinked to focus and confirmed before she came over.

"How did you know I was here?" Zenobia asked with a mix of emotions. She necessarily didn't want to go through this alone, but didn't like being followed or spied on either.

"I didn't," Penny sighed. They looked at each for a moment to process. Penny walked over to the reception desk to sign in and get her number. She took a seat next to her friend but there wasn't much to talk about. In fact, they would never talk about this day again. The day they aborted their dead boyfriend's babies.

"**W**here the heck have you been!" Callie fussed when Zenobia walked in. "And you heard from P, cuz she not answering!"

"Hey," Zenobia managed as she walked in. Penny answered the second question herself as she walked in behind her.

"Hey," Penny greeted.

"Um, hey?" Callie wondered since she rarely saw these two this subdued. Both slinked their separate ways and into their separate rooms. They climbed into their separate beds to sleep off the long day. They were both given Oxy and prescriptions for more to heal from the ordeal. She shrugged her shoulders and went about her business.

"I thought I heard Z 'ndem?" Dominique asked when she made it out to the empty living room.

"Ndem tho? Z rubbing off on you too!" Callie cackled and cracked her up as well.

"Girl she's gonna have me sounding like Miss Ceily in a minute. M-i-s-t-e-r, mista," she acted out like in the movie. The ensuing laughter was short lived when the doorbell began to chime. They both looked to the other to see which one was expecting company. Neither was so Callie slipped on her mean mug and went to pull the door open. The Mr at the door quickly erased the scowl from her face and replaced it with fear.

"The fuck you doing here B!" Callie barked since she wasn't scared of anyone. Growing up in New York City has an effect on people. It makes them either afraid of everything or afraid of nothing. She was the latter and fucking fearless. Which can actually be a dangerous trait.

"I'm here to make you rich," Mike said as he walked in on top of her. Callie had no choice but to step aside so she wouldn't get stepped on.

"Pluh-leeze nigga! My artist wouldn't sign with you if you were the last record company on earth!" Dominique barked.

"Shit, I might just be last since Jew boy got himself killed," he laughed.

"I know you did that shit! Remember, I know lots of shit!" Dominique warned. Indeed she did since she knew about the bodies he dropped in the dope game.

"Of course you do, codefendant!" he chuckled. She was a party to some of his crimes and couldn't tell if she wanted to. "Anyway, I had nothing to do with it. He and Lil Bruh had some beef, about something. I think the white boy tried him up on some gay shit or something?"

"Whatever, but like my manager said, no deal!" Callie said and piped down to match Dominique's new mood.

"A'ight, you forgot I always get what I want," he shrugged and walked away.

"Fuck 'outa here," Callie snarled as she locked the door behind him. "How the fuck he even know where we stay?"

"He makes it his business to know everything about everyone," she replied and kept watch on the door in case he came back.

"Well, at least that's over," Callie sighed and leaned back.

"Far from over. No way he gives up that easily," Dominique said, still watching the door.

"I'm about to run out," Dominique announced as she breezed through the living room.

"Un-uh, hold up! Where are you going, all cute!" Callie wanted to know. Especially since she tried to rush by without being seen. "Hot date?"

"Business actually," she replied since it was a mix of both. Definitely some business but she planned to enjoy it.

"Want me to come? Them chicks still mourning," she sighed. Neither Penny or Zenobia had ventured out of their respective rooms lately. Both were still popping Oxy and recuperating from their abortions. Physically they were better, the mental wounds would take longer to heal. Except popping pills to heal emotionally was the equivalent of peeling a scab every time it begins to heal.

"Nah, I got this. Once this is done it's full steam ahead!" Dominique declared and turned to leave.

"Yeah," Callie mused and twisted her lips as she looked down the lonely hall. She missed her girls even though they were just feet away.

Dominique drove the same route she drove so many times before. She arrived at her destination and hitched a ride into the building with a resident. She looked like she belonged so he didn't mind holding the door for her.

"Thank you," she nodded and headed down to the bank

of elevators. They nodded again when the door opened to let him out first. She rode up to her floor and got out. Her lips twisted at her own plan and all the things that could go wrong. It wasn't the brightest plan, but had to be done. She reached the door, inhaled, exhaled and rang the doorbell.

"You're early!" Savage announced when he pulled the door open. His eyes went wide when he registered the surprise. "Dominique?"

"What, don't want to see me?" she asked and looked past him to the empty sofa. It being empty was a relief but he was obviously expecting company.

"No. I mean, no I don't, don't want to see you. I thought, I mean..." he stammered as she stepped in.

"Well tell her, something else came up," she purred seductively as she brushed against his crotch on the way.

"I um, we was supposed to..." he vacillated between which vagina to indulge in. Dominique was more of a conquest than the coed he invited over. Not to mention she obviously overcame his treachery since she was back for more dick. A smug look came over his face as he nodded at what the dick does and made the call. "Hey, yeah no, something came up. Can I get a raincheck? OK, that'll work."

"Will she live?" Dominique asked when he hung up from rescheduling his booty call.

"She will, but Ion know about you," he said as he pulled his shirt over his head.

"I'll be fine," she assured him and began to strip as well. A flashback of the agents making fun of their love making on this same sofa came back to mind. "Let's go to the bed!"

"Oh, you tryna fuck-fuck!" he nodded and led the way. His dick bobbed to life with each step from the anticipation. Those young girls had nothing on this grown woman.

Savage usually started in the middle and tonight was no exception. He made himself comfortable between her legs and got to licking until her legs started kicking. That made him double down until she bust a nut in his mouth.

"You gonna return the flavor..." he asked as she sucked her own flavor off his lips.

"When we get back," she said and reached for the bowl of condoms he kept at his bedside.

"OK," he said, agreeing to go wherever since it came with some head. He looked down as she rolled the rubber on his dick and guided him inside of her.

"Don't play with it!" she demanded and pulled her legs up by the backs of her knees. Something else no man needs to have repeated.

Savage poked around for a second to find his stroke. He set his feet as he lifted up on his arms and gave her the business. All of it until she was coming every few strokes. That good, gushy pussy finally got the best of him as well.

"Fuck!" Savage grunted like a savage and went stiff as he filled the condom to the rim.

"That's it baby," she cooed and rubbed his back and he struggled for breath. As soon as he caught it, it was time to get going. "Get up baby. We're gonna be late."

"Late? Where are we going?" he asked as she pushed him up.

"I need you to make a run with me," she answered,

without actually answering. "Let's hurry so I can taste that dick."

Savage was indeed a savage and rushed into the bathroom to flush the rubber, wash his dick and get dressed. He came back just as Dominique finished getting dressed. She shot a text out as they left the condo to let her people know she was on the way. Savage rambled about something or another as they rode.

"Mmhm. Un-huh. Ki-ki-ki," she hummed and giggled to whatever he was saying since far heavier subjects weighed on her whole soul. Savage rambled on happily, like a broad until they pulled off the highway at Candler road. It was one of the places bougie blacks tried to avoid.

"Where did you say we were going again?" he asked as if she had told him before. She hadn't and that's what she replied.

"I didn't," she said but the sign they drove by said East-wyck Apartments. She drove down the hill, around to the left and into a parking spot. "Come on."

"Where?" he asked before budging but she was already out of the car. He didn't see anyone else so he sighed and got out. Men have jumped through more hoops than this to get their dick sucked so he fell in step with her. A few steps later young men came out from different directions. Savage wanted to run but the assault rifles in their hands said it wouldn't help. He reached for his wallet and handed it to the closest thug.

"Ion want your fuck ass money fuck nigga!" the kids snarled and slapped it away. Some junky would come up when he came upon it later because they weren't here for his money.

"This him?" one of the young men asked with his chopper facing Savage's feet.

"Yup. Ask him," she dared and cocked her head.

"Ask me what!" Savage pleaded. If a question and answer would get him out of whatever this was he was ready to be asked.

"If you the police?" the teen growled as the barrel came up to his midsection.

"Tell him you're the snitch who put the folks on the girls!" Dominique snapped and slapped a spark out of his cheek. "Tell em Vaughn ain't had shit to do with this!"

"They said I was going to get raped!" Savage shouted and squeezed his butt cheeks together at the mention. It was the right answer for Dominique who stepped out of the line of fire. Just in the nic of time since the kid fired a few rounds that ripped through his torso.

Savage went down as the others stepped up. The teens were fueled by anger and sorrow for killing their own for something he didn't do. Young Vaughn was gone but Savage was going with him. They all stepped up and fired on the wounded man.

"Damn!" Dominique exclaimed as the sounds of gun fire continued even after she had pulled away. It stopped when their clips ran dry but only for as long as it took to insert fresh ones. Her head shook as she drove out of the complex. It wouldn't bring Young Vaughn back but it was still justice. She turned the radio on to drown out her thoughts as she drove home. The DJ played Young Vaughn and Lil Bruh songs back to back since they joined the legion of dead rappers on the radio. Once the songs went off he rambled through the city's upcoming events.

'Y'all join us Saturday night for the *real pretty thugs performing live!'* he said to her surprise.

It was a surprise even though Penny and Zenobia had their own management. Still, she and Jovita agreed to work together going forward. She picked up her phone to check on the disconnect but it was already ringing with Jovita's name on the screen.

"Um, did you forget my number girlfriend?" Jovita asked cordially. She tried to mask her attitude with the pet name but it still seeped through around the edges.

"I was wondering the same thing? Especially when I just heard the girls are supposed to be performing this weekend?" Dominique asked. There was a brief moment of silence as they made matching faces on their sides of the call.

"Wait, so you didn't book them?" Jovita asked. This time the confusion rang through loud and clear.

"No! I thought you did!" she shot back. Another moment of silence then, "Meet me at the apartment!"

CHAPTER 10

"Looks who came back from the dead," Callie announced and instantly regretted her choice of words. "I mean, you were asleep, for like..."

"Days. It's cool. I know what you meant," Penny sighed. She had finally accepted her new life and the fact that Ethan would not be in it. She had gotten used to losing the people she loved and that was just fucked up. She tucked the rest of her Oxy subscription into her nightstand and was determined to stand on her own.

Callie just sighed since she too had gotten numb to loss. She once heard that whatever doesn't kill you will only make you stronger. She was Hercules by now from all the trauma and drama in her short life. Now she was ready to win. They were a signature away from riches to match their fame. The recent rash of violence was a dual edged sword. They added a few hundred thousand more followers but a couple of the labels had withdrawn their contract offers.

Ethan's company was the top runner but now didn't have the money he offered as a signing bonus. Jovita needed to use every cent they had to promote the new album. She would pay the girls what Ethan promised once Young Vaughn's insurance paid out. Ethan's millions would go to Arial.

"Hey y'all," Zenobia greeted when she emerged. Callie braced herself for her infectious sadness but she seemed much better today. Almost, happy.

"Hey girl!" Callie cheered and stopped short of asking how she was feeling. She looked like she was in a better mood so she would leave it like that.

"We supposed to be doing a show this weekend?" she asked, looking between the two. Callie and Penny looked at each other for the answer that neither one had. On cue the door opened for Dominique and Jovita walked in. Both breathed fire as they worked their phones. They both hung up in frustration.

"What?" Callie asked on behalf of the rest.

"We got a show?" Zenobia added and danced to the music in her head. Her friends paused at her odd behavior, then shrugged it off just as quickly. At least she wasn't hiding in her room, under her comforter anymore.

"That's what we're trying to ascertain," Jovita said as she made another call.

"We didn't book it?" Dominique asked since it wasn't totally uncommon for an artist to book a show on their own. None of them answered since it was news to them as well.

"Voicemail again!" Jovita groaned.

"How much we getting paid?" Penny asked. Callie and Zenobia tuned in as well since they had no clue as to what was going on.

"No less than twenty, but we didn't book this show," Dominique replied.

"No, we didn't but I'm thinking more like thirty. Once the album drops," Jovita added to the girl's delight.

"Like, thousand?" Zenobia exclaimed. They used to pay thirty dollars to watch a show, now they would be getting thirty thousand to perform one.

"Yes, thirty thousand," Dominique answered them both before asking a question of her own. "Think we should just show up?"

"Yeah and if they don't have the money we will just leave. Let them deal with the angry crowd," the other manager said and it was set.

"I'm on some thug shit tonight!" Callie declared as she stomped out in a pair of pink Timberland boots. A pair of tight jeans showed off the fat ass and a pink Yankees jersey was tied at her belly to add a little sexy.

"Facts! I'm on my Atl shit too!" Zenobia agreed. She too was dressed for whatever since it was still unclear who booked a show for them without knowing it. She matched Callie's athletic theme, except she had a Braves jersey over her tight jeans and K-swiss on her feet. A Braves hat tilted to the side completed the look. The Oxy flowing through her system gave her a warm glow.

"Awe man!" Penny moaned when she came out and saw she was way, way over dressed. She was killing it in the tiny dress and big heels. She was both overdressed and under-dressed at the same time since a titty fell out when she spun around to go change.

"Mmhm, see!" Zenobia teased as she tucked the runaway breast back into her dress.

"Where's Penny?" Dominique asked as she came from her room. It was clear she was on the same page since she was cute in some chino pants and sneakers. Her attire was business but still casual enough to kick someone in the mouth if need be.

"Went to change," Callie said as she went to open the door. "Sup Jovita."

"Hey. Y'all ready?" Jovita replied and asked eagerly. She nodded at the rugged outfits but missed their point. She was thinking photo shoot, they were thinking about throwing some hands.

"May as well get you a key shawty," Zenobia greeted as the woman stepped in.

"Better?" Penny asked when she returned rocking her Dodger's blue and a pair of Chuck's.

"Much, Snoop Dog!" Callie cackled and they all headed out.

"We're riding together!" Dominique decided for them all when Jovita pulled her keys from her purse. There was no question mark in her comment so no one questioned her.

They loaded into the Range Rover with the managers up front and the group leaned back in the back seat.

"Go live," Jovita suggested as they cruised through downtown Atlanta. The girls got hyped at the idea and Zenobia pulled up the group's IG to put on for their growing fans.

"Yoooo! Pretty Thugs in thi bih!" Z-money shouted into the camera. She panned to her sides so her girls could add, "P-muhfucking-money! The Harlem hitter, C-money up in this piece!"

"A thousand damn viewers already!" Jovita was trying to say but it had doubled by the time she reached the end of her sentence. It would be up to fifty thousand by the time they reached the club. They were still clowning and chatting with their fans when they pulled up to the packed venue. Some of the IG followers were actually in the long line to get in to see them.

"Pretty Thugs," Jovita confirmed when she read the sign on the marquee. She squinted when she caught something else in the sign. "Wait, real Pretty Thugs?"

"I see?" Dominique asked when she read it too. They didn't have to wait long for an answer when Mike's Maybach whipped past them and stopped at the valet. Time slowed to a crawl like a slow motion shot in a video. Mike was all pearly white smile and glittering diamonds as he stepped out. The hired photographers snapped pictures causing his jewelry to flash brilliantly. Then came the girls. First a light skin, followed by a cute darker toned woman, and finally a white girl with an artificial looking tan.

"That's right!" the real Pretty Thugs!" he announced as they posed along with him.

"Oh hell to the naw!" Penny declared and pulled the door handle. Zenobia tossed the phone down while they were still live but Jovita quickly snatched it up and pointed as they marched up to the entrance.

"Dats rat! Ki-ki, from the original Pretty Thugs and we..." the white girl was saying through her gold grill before the make believe Callie corrected her.

"Real..." Jersey Girl reminded and let the leader continue while the faux Z-money called Country Girl nodded. Mike had adopted the name but added 'real' since Penny, Callie and Zenobia were the originals. He hoped they would feed off the bullshit since the masses love the bullshit.

"That's right, my bad. The real Pretty Thugs! Don't be fooled by no imitations!" The fake P-money stated.

"The fuck y'all got going on!" Zenobia snapped furiously when they made it up to the front. Penny and Callie were no talk, all smoke. They wanted to fight, not debate.

"Security!" Mike laughed and was quickly surrounded by large men. "They don't come in!"

"What the fuck are you up to Mike!" Dominique shouted after them as they disappeared into the club. Penny tried to lead the charge behind them but the men held them back.

"Fuck that, these people came to see us!" Callie said, pointing to the confused crowd. The club owner had held the line to make the club appear full but it was about to back-fire. Only half the people made it inside and the other half weren't going anywhere now.

"Well give them a show then!" Jovita shouted as she captured the footage live.

"Word!" Dominique added and jumped back inside of her truck. She rolled down all the windows and blasted the album through the premium sound system.

"Come on y'all!" Z-money announced and climbed atop the Range Rover. Her friends joined her as they tried to run through the entire album. They were soon surrounded by their audience.

"The fuck Mike?" the club owner needed to know when his line abruptly died on the sidewalk. "You said these chicks were them chicks?"

"No I didn't! I said, the real. Now start the fucking show!" he barked and shoved the man away. "Get your asses on stage and turn that shit out!"

"But..." the supposed to be Zenobia fussed since she knew they weren't ready. Mike put the group of girls he was fucking together in a few weeks and recorded an album. Lil Bruh had already written a slew of ratchet songs about selling pussy and sucking dicks when Mike was still hoping to sign the real Pretty Thugs. When he couldn't he found the ringers and put it together. He just needed to beat the real Pretty Thugs to market. They may have been worse but they were first and that would pay off.

"But my ass!" he said and gave her a kick in her ass to get her going. The crowd was mixed since the beats were banging but they weren't what they came for. Even Mike wasn't very impressed as the impostors twerked and worked the stage.

Mike noticed people checking their phones and rushing outside. His group was only halfway through their first song when they lost half their audience. He pulled out his own phone and saw what the problem was.

"These bitches!" he growled even though he had to admire it. Still, he grabbed his security to go outside and fuck up the show. They stepped out and found a full concert on the top of a Range Rover.

"When I say Pretty, y'all say thugs!" Callie shouted through her hands. "Pretty...Thugs!"

The crowd responded to the back and forth chant between songs. They didn't have mics so they just yelled along to their own music. Nor could they do any of the dances they made up in the tight space but didn't need to since the video of The Money Dance had a million views. By the time the song came on the crowd was all doing their dance.

"Break that shit up!" Mike demanded. His hired help moved forward to do just that but the club owner had already called the police for the same reason. He made no money from the party on the sidewalk.

"Twelve!" people began to shout when several police cars whipped up from different directions.

"Hold up. Let po-po handle it," Mike decided and called his men off.

Cops of different demographics filed out of the cop cars by twos to investigate the disturbance. White, black, young, old, male and female. The middle aged white sergeant twisted his lips as he tried to ascertain the situation. He finally figured it out when Young Vaughn's song featuring the Pretty Thugs came on next.

"Oh that's my jam!" the sergeant declared and tried his best to do the Money Dance.

"That ain't it sarge!" a black, lady cop announced and showed him how it was done. Most of the cops danced along with the music while the others made sure to record it. This was a public relations gold mine in the making. Clips would go viral and make the national nightly news.

"Are you getting this!" Dominique pleaded.

"Am I!" Jovita exclaimed. The live was quickly nearing a million viewers and the crowd on the sidewalk grew just as quickly.

"A-yo! Pretty Thug's debut album, Pretty Thuggin, coming soon!" Callie shouted and the crowd cheered. They cheered even louder when P-money dived into the crowd. The crowd caught her and passed her down the sidewalk.

"I ain't finna do all that!" Zenobia laughed as she climbed down.

"Word!" Penny agreed and climbed down behind her. They spent the next hour taking pics with fans and securing their future. That included wearing the police hats and taking pics on their cop cars.

"The fuck was this bull shit?" Dominique asked when she approached Mike. Ironically she felt more sorrow than anger because this was just sad.

"Free country. Built off competition," he shrugged and watched the real Pretty Thugs embrace the moment.

"Yeah but their name too? They were calling themselves that even before we came along," she reminded.

"And, my girls are gonna ride off that wave. We can both eat! Controversy sells!" Mike nodded with himself.

"Like Young Vaughn and Lil Bruh huh?" Dominique offered before offering her back as she walked away.

CHAPTER 11

"Mmhm. Mmhm. OK then. Damn!" Dominique hummed and cheered as she read over the record contract. There is literally tons of money to be made from a successful album and most labels literally didn't want the artist to have any of it.

Ethan had money so he wasn't motivated by greed. His love of music moved him to start his own label. He would let the artist get the lion share and still make plenty of money. The label ate off the sales but left shows and merchandise alone. Unlike the 360 deals that charged the artist with the Vaseline they used to fuck them.

"Yeah, I know," Jovita nodded. She didn't need to read the contract for her clients since she helped craft them. "Ethan was a fair man."

"And we're going to make him proud!" Penny declared and signed by the space reading, Penelope Manning.

Zenobia took the pen from her hand and signed next to her own name. All eyes were on Callie.

"Let's get it!" she proclaimed and snatched the pen. Jovita smiled as the group was now official. Their phones had been ringing nonstop since the viral live from the night before. They reached just over two million viewers from all over the world.

"Oh! It's Zarah from the clothing company!" Dominique cheered but that's all.

"You not going to answer it!" Callie shrieked in shock and for good reason. The offer was a million dollar deal for five years.

"Eventually..." she said. Her phone rang again and she twisted her lips as she held the screen up to show Callie the woman had called back once again.

"Answer it!" she pleaded.

"Hello?" Dominique asked with a mock attitude and rolled her eyes. She listened carefully but ad-libbed with a few, 'Mmhm' and 'Un-huh'. So pretty much the original deal? Before they got over a million worldwide views for a live..."

Callie couldn't take it so she stepped out on the balcony. A million dollar deal for a Harlem orphan was more than she could process. Plus the fact she liked their clothing. She spent good money on the brand but now the brand wanted to pay her good money to wear their clothing.

"Callie!" Dominique called as she held her hand over the receiver, before resuming the call. Callie returned just as she wrapped up the call. "I don't represent them, but I will give you their manager's name and number. Keep in mind, they have offers so come correct!"

"Well?" Callie asked and winced to brace herself for the answer.

"Well, she came back with that same lame ass offer. A million dollars for five years," she said and rolled eyes and flipped her hair to show what she thought of it.

"And!" she bounced from excitement. The thought of actually turning down a million dollars was very confusing to her.

"And I turned her ass down!" she snapped. A loud gasp escaped all three thugs just like Dominique expected. She waited another second before continuing. "Then agreed to two million for the same period!"

"Dang!" Zenobia declared at her friend becoming a millionaire right in front of her eyes.

"So, I'm getting a check for two million dollars?" Callie dared.

"No chica. Not quite," Dominique laughed then went on to explain the terms of the deal. After her twenty percent Callie would receive monthly payments of twenty six thousand dollars. "That's before taxes. We have to find you a good accountant!"

"Tuh!" Zenobia huffed at the thought of paying taxes. Especially state taxes since the neighborhood she grew up in was so fucked up. It was the same state so how could Buckhead look so dramatically different from Bankhead.

"It's Jovita!" Penny announced when her phone buzzed

in her lap. She was about to call her anyway but she beat her to it.

"Put her on speaker!" Zenobia instructed since she was a part of any conversation. "Hello!"

"Hey girl!" Jovita smiled through the line. "Where's Z?"

"I'm here!" Zenobia leaned in and announced.

"Good. Cuz I got some news for you both! I was on the line with One Ummah clothing when Zarah from Iqra Ink called. I merged the calls so they could hear each other's offers!" she cheered.

"Wow!" Zenobia reeled when she heard they had a multi million dollar deal with One Ummah.

"Wow!" Callie added since it was more than she received but she wasn't hating. As long as they were all winning she didn't mind. She judged her pockets from themselves, not anyone else's.

"But, there's more!" Jovita added. "Let's do lunch so we can lay it all out!"

The girls agreed and scrambled to get dressed. Dominique's phone rang a few seconds later.

"Hey girl! Congrats," Dominique greeted. She added a little extra cheer in her tone to mask the jealousy in her heart. It was a competitive jealousy without a trace of hate for hate's sake.

"Naw, ain't no congrats sis. That was some gangster ass shit you did, putting me on with Zarah!" she said since it made One Ummah come correct and top their offer.

"Cuz, it ain't about us ma! As long as these girls win I'm Gucci!" Dominique declared. She had the benefit of a mother and father and still made mistakes. Mistakes she would try her best to keep all three from making. She and Callie were the closest on the surface but she loved them all.

"That's what the heck I'm talmbout!" Jovita shot back.

"Oh hell, Zenobia got you too I see!" she laughed. Zenobia's southern slang was so infectious she had them all speaking it.

"Well I'm finna get dressed so we can do lunch. We gotta talk about tour dates. It's on!" she cheered and hung up.

"Wow!" Zenobia exclaimed as they walked into Barakah's Halal. She had lived in this city her whole life and had never been to its finest eatery.

"No wow!" Jovita semi chided. "This is your new life! Get used to it!"

"Our new life. Penny been 'bout this life," Callie reminded.

"On someone else's dime. Believe me it hit different when you earn your own bread," Penny advised. Jovita nodded in agreement since she too came from bread but was now a baker herself and made her own bread.

"P-money said that!" Dominique applauded then got serious. "Shit comes with responsibilities!"

"Taxes, we know," Callie sighed and twisted her lips. Being single put her into the forty percent tax bracket and she didn't like that one bit.

"Please, pay your taxes! I'll get you all a good accountant,"

Jovita said and looked over to Dominique since she meant Callie too. She gave a slight nod that contained her blessings. "Now, I have some paperwork for you all."

The waitress came for drink orders as Jovita passed contracts around the table. Both Penny and Zenobia accepted their paperwork to become Spokespersons for One Ummah clothing. Callie tilted her head when she received a contract as well.

"They want the whole group," Jovita explained. It might make up for the deals on the table exclusively for P-money.

"I know they don't want me too? I mean, auntie is still fine but..." Dominique reeled when Jovita slid a contract her way as well. Her brows bunched when she read the heading. "Word?"

"Word! The new vice president of the company," Jovita explained.

"So, I work for you?" she huffed.

"Not if you don't want to. I mean..." Jovita said, sounding wounded.

"I'm just kidding! Hell yeah!" she agreed and quickly signed. She was usually more astute but didn't even bother to read it. Whatever it was, was far more than she got from Mike.

"Now, the work begins! Video shoot tomorrow. Photo shoot for the album cover. Photo shoots for your contracts, appearance, show..." Jovita rattled off. "I hope you ladies got a good night's sleep last night. Because it'll be your last for a while!"

"What about dude and his imposter group?" Dominique wondered.

"Legal says there's nothing we can do about the name," she sighed. "We just need to ignore them. They beat us to the market and have an advantage."

"They shit wack tho!" Callie fussed and scrunched her face up. They were the same lame songs Lil Bruh tried to give her when he was recruiting for Mike.

"And they ugly!" Penny added with a grimace.

"And they hoes!" Zenobia tossed in her two cents as she pulled up the real Pretty Thugs IG account. "And they talking shit!"

"And they're gaining on us!" Dominique added when she looked at their followers. They were still a few hundred thousand followers behind but controversy sells records.

"Fucking Mike," Callie sighed and shook her head.

"Fuck Mike and fuck them hoes!" Penny declared and was done with it.

"I'm pretty sure that's exactly what he's doing..." Dominique surmised correctly.

"Ooh I like these!" White girl Ki-ki proclaimed when she saw the foam wedge on the middle of the bed. It wasn't the kind from the orthopedic doctor to keep a patient elevated. This came from the sex shop to help hold that ass up in different sexual positions. It helped mimic the perfect angle for precision back shots for women who didn't naturally have that arch in their back.

"Yeah," Mike grunted as he came out of his clothes as well. He watched the sexy white girl get naked but still had a soft dick by the time he joined her. She laid over the wedge and offered her pinkness like a lamb on an altar. He had to fondle it a little and it soaked his hand but still, "I had something else in mind."

"Huh? Oh, OK," Ki-ki said when he flipped her over on her back. Now her head was elevated in the perfect position for her to watch him eat her out. But, that's not where he was going with it either.

Instead he mounted her face as her mouth opened wide like a baby bird waiting to be fed. He fed her too and dropped his now semi erect dick on her tongue.

She worked her white girl magic and soon had a full fledged hard on in her mouth. Ki-ki had a mean head game but again, Mike had other plans. He began to slowly stroke her face. Only for a few strokes before it got good to him.

'Gawk! Gawk! Gawk!' her throat announced with each down stroke. Tears streamed from her eyes as he assaulted her larynx and esophagus.

"Fuck!" Mike proclaimed as he fucked her mouth like a vagina. He reached back and fondled her juice box at the same time. Mike felt a nut stirring and dug down deeper into her windpipe. She gawked even louder as her eyes fluttered from being choked with the dick. Luckily for her he couldn't take it much longer. He pushed to the limits of her throat and exploded.

Ki-ki's eyes watered as he skeeted down her throat. She didn't have the aged old dilemma whether to swallow or spit since he deposited them babies right into her stomach.

"Augghh!" she gasped when he extracted the dick from her respiratory system. She inhaled and exhaled freely and caught her breath. It wasn't over though since he flipped her over on the wedge.

Her vagina was plump and swollen from the excitement and it would have been a crime to let it go to waste. Mike may have been a criminal at heart but abided by the law tonight. He leaned in and sucked a nut out of that box from the back. She was still reeling and writhing from pleasure when he roughly shoved back inside of her.

Her gushy vagina hugged him like a mother's love but there would be no tenderness tonight. Mike positioned his muscular arms on the bed and lifted on his tippy toes. His back hunched like a horny German Sheppard as he fucked the daylights out the white girl.

Mike would have loved to have Penny folded over the wedge just as much as he would like to have signed them. His 'real Pretty Thugs' would have to do in and out of his bed. The budding controversy was working and his less talented group was making some noise. Only because again, people are some bullshit and like to see bullshit. The same bullshit that got Young Vaughn and Lil Bruh elaborate funerals. Young Dolph, Tupac, Freaky Tye, Jam Master Jay, The Notorious...

That too was a win since the insurance payout would come through shortly. Plus the album was selling and songs were playing on the radio, generating royalties he would keep. He thought about killing this white girl he was in just to collect another quick payout. He laughed the thought away since another nut was rushing up from his toes.

Mike thought about flipping her back over and coming in her mouth again so he could keep his kids together. That required pulling out of this hot, tight, wet vagina and that just wasn't happening. Instead he pushed down to the bottom of her barrel and blasted off inside of her.

"Fuck!" Mike grunted and struggled for breath as he rolled off the bed.

"Want some more head!" Ki-ki offered since she aimed to please.

"Nah, I'm good. For now," he huffed and looked up at the ceiling. These imitation Pretty Thugs were OK, still he wanted the real deal. He looked up at the ceiling as he plotted his next move.

Mike rolled off the bed and left the white girl sleeping and slobbering. He headed into his office and dumped a pile of cocaine on his desk. He coarsely chopped it up and made a few lines. Big lines that he quickly inhaled up each nostril.

"Conyo!" Mike reeled like scarface and fell back in his chair. And just like Tony he was coked up and not thinking straight. "You wanna go to war! War it is!"

CHAPTER 12

"**A**we man!" Zenobia reeled as she searched her room. It was bad enough that she had to wake up at five am so they could be on set by six. Shooting a video in a booming club meant doing it in the morning since it would be packed at night. A bunch of extras were eating breakfast in local waffle shops since they just left the club an hour ago. That was all bad but even worse she couldn't find any more oxy. "I could have sworn..."

"I'm up!" Penny shouted at the knock on her door. It was the same thing she said a few minutes ago when Dominique went around to wake everyone up. She still hadn't budged so she let out a deep sigh and kicked her comforter off her legs.

"It's me," Zenobia whispered as she slipped inside the room.

"I'm up," Penny repeated almost matching her whisper but wondered why they were whispering.

"You got any more oxy?" she asked.

"Yeah, I stopped taking them shits," Penny grimaced since she didn't like taking them. She had sold enough pills to know they caused more problems than they solved.

"Let me have a few," Zenobia asked just below the whisper, like she knew she was doing something wrong.

"Girrrrl..." Penny sighed and shook her head as she dug them out. "This it tho. The last of them so..."

"I know. I'm good, just after Vaughn and Ethan and shit!" Zenobia fussed in a normal tone. She did have a lot going on but most drug addicts do. If she wasn't careful she could end up down that same road.

"Yeah," Penny said and twisted her lips. The excuse sounded so good she almost took one back for herself.

"Let's get it ladies!" Dominique announced as she came through tapping on doors again. Luckily each bedroom had a bathroom which cut down on time. It was nearly six am when they finally pulled out and headed over to the club.

"Dang!" Zenobia declared when they arrived and saw all the people milling about. Besides the director and his film crew there were hundreds of extras hanging around. In addition were literally a hundred armed security guards to protect the group. Jovita wasn't taking any chances. The security bill was still less than a funeral cost.

"Hey ladies!" the director Moshe cheered and looked down at his watch. The consummate professional didn't like being kept waiting. "Hair and make-up! Let's get this show on the road!"

"What's first?" Jovita asked. Dominique leaned in as he showed them his vision board for the shoot. "Looks great!"

"Looks expensive!" Dominique worried.

"Perfection isn't cheap!" Moshe huffed and switched away.

"Atl!" Jovita laughed. There were plenty of girly men in the city and on the set. "Gotta spend money to make money!"

"True. Mike's cheap ass was always looking to cut corners and cheat people," she recalled.

"Well, we'll have cut a corner or two to launch this album right but the debut video sets the tone," she explained.

After hair and makeup the girls took the stage to run through a mock performance. They lip synced to the song a few times to get different angles and shots. Then had a make believe party in the VIP section, sipping make believe champagne.

Dominique had ran a Money Dance contest on their IG account. The winners got a chance to be in the video. They got good footage of the winners performing their signature dance. The group joined and made an impromptu Soul Train line that even their managers had to join in.

"Cut! That's a wrap ladies and gentlemen!" Moshe finally announced.

"Good, cuz I'm 'hangry!" Callie growled. She had snacked off the buffet line setup for the crew but was ready for a whole meal.

"You should be. It's eight damn o'clock!" Zenobia fussed when she saw the time was some fourteen hours later.

"Get used to it ladies. This is the business part of the music business," Jovita explained. "Get food, get rest, tomorrow is another busy day!"

"Photo shoot at noon!" Dominique announced.

"Good! Cuz I got something to do in the morning!" Zenobia huffed. They left the club and headed over to S&S Chicken and Waffles. The owner had offered free food for life in exchange for posting on their social media. A win/win since they got extra exposure. Plus the group won since that shit is delicious!

"**W**here you finna go?" Callie asked when Zenobia emerged from her room fully dressed. She had been looking in the packed fridge trying to decide what to eat but if she was going out she could bring food back when she returned.

"To see a man about a mule. Literally," she laughed. She knew her friend was hungry though so she invited her to tag along. "Come with?"

"Five minutes!" Callie said and took off down the hall.

"What y'all got going on?" Penny yawned as she came out of her room. She was already awake but the heavy footsteps brought her out to investigate.

"Finna see a mule!" Callie replied over her shoulder as she rushed into her room to squeeze into a pair of jeans and sneakers.

"I wanna see a mule!" Penny pouted.

"It's not a, oh come on!" Zenobia agreed and shook her head. This mission needed to be done but didn't mind having company. A few minutes later they headed for the door.

"Photo shoot at twelve ladies!" Dominique called from her room when she heard them all leaving.

"I'll drive!" both Penny and Callie offered since neither liked riding in Zenobia's older car anymore than she liked driving it.

"Nah, I gotta drive," she insisted and lifted her chin.

"Backseat!" Callie and Penny both called out. Usually people vie for the front seat but a spring poked out from it. They cackled as they both climbed into the back seat.

"Mmhm," Zenobia hummed and twisted her lips. The old car did seem to get older by the day. She had a trick for them as soon as they reached their destination. In the meanwhile they checked their social media accounts where more views and likes translated into more money. Also to keep an eye on the competition since the imposters had pages as well.

"OK then!" Callie cheered as her likes neared a hundred thousand for her most recent pic. Iqra Ink paid a bonus for any sales made through the link on her page.

"Get money!" P-money sang and danced at her own likes and comments. Then went to check the dick pics in her DM. They all used to get random dick pics from random dudes, but now millionaire rappers were all showing their dicks for some strange reason.

"See what these rats 'talmbout..." Callie said as she went to check the so-called real Pretty Thugs page. As soon as she logged into the official page she realized the group had been tagged.

'P-money ain't got shit on Ki-ki! We both white but I got the moves!' the wannabe P-money called White girl Ki-ki announced and began to twerk to one of their songs.

'Facts cuz Z-money will never be Country Girl' Zenobia's double declared and began to clap her booty cheeks. Jersey Girl was supposed to be Callie to match the up top vibe so she began grinding and hunching in the air.

"Bet that twerk wind smells like octopus croquettes!" Penny laughed. "That air is prolly flammable!"

The fake group was too funny to take seriously so they didn't even respond. Dominique already informed them that Mike needed the controversy to hype his group. The Pretty Thugs were already a movement.

"Man, fuck them hoes!" Zenobia declared triumphantly as she pulled into her destination.

"OK then," Penny nodded in agreement at the upscale car dealership.

"You're up Jonathan!" the sales manager said when the car pulled up. He made them rotate each time a customer pulled in to keep things fair.

"Sheesh!" the man groaned when he saw the jalopy they pulled in with and assumed they didn't have any money.

"Don't judge a book by it's cover," the owner called from his cubicle. He liked to be hands on with his employees so he had a desk on the sales floor with the rest of them.

"At least my food won't get too cold," Jonathan said and took a last bite of his food. His hopes went even lower when he saw the young girls getting out of the car. He let out a sigh and pasted a faux smile on his tanned face. He saw three girls but the racist only registered one. "Can I help you?"

"Me? No," Penny replied. "My sister is buying."

"Sister!" he reeled, then nodded since Zenobia was nearly as light. "Mom caught a slight case of jungle fever I see!"

"The fuck?" Callie grimaced at the remark. His light hearted laugh was meant to dilute the racist remark but didn't.

"You sure this is the right place?" Penny asked. "Cuz this fool..."

"Mmhm, and there it is!" Callie said and took off towards the car she had found online. There were plenty of convertible Benzes in the city of Atlanta but this one was hers.

"Um, that's eighty thousand!" Jonathan stressed, then felt a need to expound. "Dollars."

"As opposed to pesos?" Callie quipped.

"Nah, he means food stamps," Penny snapped and marched inside. All eyes were on her when she came into the office and looked around. "Excuse me, who is the manager!"

"I am but he's the owner," the man laughed as he threw his boss under the bus.

"I might be the manager too..." the man sniped since he was doing the manager's job and came over. "Ervin Clayton. I'm the owner."

"And your salesman out there is a racist!" Penny pouted and pointed.

"He doesn't like white people?" Ervin asked in confusion since Jonathan was as white as she was.

"Oh you got jokes huh?" she shot back and twisted her lips.

"How about I take care of you personally?" he offered and followed her outside. Which allowed him a good look at her ass as they went. It was doing it's own dance just from walking. They arrived just in time since Zenobia was holding Callie from jumping on the man.

"Come on Cleo! Set it off!" the salesman laughed and antagonized.

"Whoa, what's going on out here Jonathan!" Ervin boomed. It was his family name on Clayton Motorsports so he took fighting customers very personally.

"Venus Williams there got upset when I asked how her friend was supposed to pay for an eighty thousand dollar car," he shrugged like he asked all customers how they intended to pay.

"This nigga 'talmbout, y'all don't take lay away!" Callie growled and slipped away from Zenobia. She almost reached the man before the owner grabbed her.

"Whoa!" he repeated and lost his train of thought when he and Callie came face to face. "I um, I'll take care of you guys."

"I'm the one buying!" Zenobia protested since Penny and Callie kept getting all the attention.

"No problem. Let's take her for a drive," the owner suggested and nodded at his employee. "Grab the keys."

"Chop, chop nigga!" Callie teased while Penny added, "Double time!"

"Why do you guys look so familiar?" Ervin asked.

"How can you tell?" Penny asked since he hadn't taken his eyes off Callie.

"We're the Pretty Thugs!" Zenobia proudly proclaimed and nodded his head.

"OK! You guys look even prettier in person!" he gushed and Callie blushed.

"How can you tell?" Penny repeated since he still hadn't taken his eyes off Callie.

"Thank you!" she cooed and rocked while her friends made fun of her. Luckily Jonathan returned with the keys.

"Here you go boss," Jonathan offered when he returned with the keys.

'Boss!' no one said but everyone thought. The handsome black man was only thirty but the fifty year old white man was calling him boss. That was more attractive than the tailored suit he wore.

"Take it for a drive!" Ervin said and handed Zenobia the keys. She rushed behind the wheel while Penny jumped into the passenger seat.

"You're letting them take an eighty thousand dollar car out alone?" Jonathan reeled at the breach of protocols.

"They cool. If they don't come back I'll keep her," Ervin said and walked away with his new friend Callie.

CHAPTER 13

"This is it!" Callie sighed and shook her head. The first single was already at number three on Atlanta radio charts but tonight was the official album release party.

"We did that shit C-money!" Penny acknowledged and knocked away a tear.

"Y'all did that!" Dominique clapped. "I knew y'all were stars from the moment I saw you!"

"No, you thought we wanted yo rusty ass man!" Callie cracked and cracked them all up.

"Speaking of rusty ass men, I hope he don't brang his rusty ass around the club tonight!" Zenobia fussed when she came through the front door.

"The heck you been?" Callie wanted to know since it was time to get dressed and head out. They didn't want to be late to their own party.

"Had to check on granny," she replied quickly since it was true. So true she had no need to add the part about copping some Xany from the hood while she was there. Granny had a pill plug of her own and hooked her up.

"How is she?" Callie asked while Penny added, "You should have brought her!"

"Shit, she wanted to come," she laughed. They kicked it for a few more minutes before getting up to go get dressed. They weren't actually performing tonight so the focus was on cute over comfort.

"Now comes the hard part!" Callie groaned as she stepped into her room. Iqra Ink had sent racks and racks of clothes for her to choose from. Her bedroom had more clothes than the closet did.

She made it easy on herself by selecting the new pink Prada pumps she bought. That cut the choices down dramatically since she had to match the color. She cracked a smile at the thought of seeing Ervin again. They texted daily since they met but busy schedules prevented them from hanging out.

"Grrrr!" Callie growled at the bad bitch in the full length mirror. She did a little jiggle to make sure her titties didn't pop out the deep plunge in her dress. She turned to the side and saw it barely covered all that ass she was toting around. "Perfect!"

"OK then!" Dominique agreed with her selection. Callie could technically wear whatever she wanted to wear but they both got paid when she wore Iqra clothing. That's why she pulled her camera to capture some pictures to upload. Getting paid to dress up was a dream job and she could not, would not pass up the easy money.

"Cha-ching. Cha-ching, cha-ching!" Callie laughed with each pose since each pic was a check. The execs at the clothing line admired how happy she always seemed in their clothes. They just didn't know why. "Cha-ching, wait...Cha-ching!"

"Y'all stooooopid!" Zenobia snickered when she came out from her room. She had a good buzz rolling through her system that made her extra happy.

"OK Gucci mama!" Dominique admired her outfit. She too made money from her post when wearing One Ummah but opted to rock Gucci pumps and a Gucci tube dress. Her fat ass and plump breast made the expensive clothes look a little more expensive.

"Un! Un! Un-huh!" she chanted as Dominique snapped some pictures of her too. Enough likes and Gucci would have to take notice and cut a check too.

"Hole up!" Penny demanded as she came out and saw the informal photoshoot. Someone might think they would get tired of taking pictures after the tens of thousands they had taken over the past few weeks. They would be wrong though because they giggled, primped and posed until Jovita used her key to enter the apartment. She had to get her own key simply because these chicks didn't like answering the door. With four people in the apartment each one still ignored the door bell so someone else could answer. Unless they ordered food, then all them bum rushed the door.

Each of them, including Dominique had more than enough money to move. Each had window shopped for houses, condos and lofts online, but no one wanted to go anywhere. Why live alone when you can live with your best friends. They all paused since Jovita was always all business, all the time.

"Let me get in here!" she laughed and joined in. Dominique set the phone on automatic and sat it down to get in on the action with the rest. They were going to be late to their own party but a party's not really a party until the Pretty Thugs fall through.

―――――

"Finally!" Zenobia rejoiced to herself as she neared the valet parking. She had been here with others but this was a first in her own car. She was all smiles when the attendant held her door open. He missed it though because he was too busy looking between her legs as she stepped out. Not that she minded when she saw where his eyes went. "That rabbit fat ain't it!"

"I'll suck that thing inside out!" the attendant declared as he got in her car and took it over to the lot.

"Dang boy!" she grimaced and laughed. "That sounds painful!"

"It's Z-money!" a woman old enough to be Zenobia's auntie screamed and fawned when she spotted her. Zenobia remembered being in those long lines trying to see her favorite artist. Sometimes she didn't even make it inside if the club was packed.

"Hey girl!" she shouted back and headed over for pictures and autographs.

"My bish," Penny laughed when she reached the valet and saw her partner in the line with their fans. She treated the attendant to another crotch shot as she got out.

"P-money!" someone shouted as she came over and joined her friend and fans. It only got better a few minutes later when C-money joined them on the sidewalk. Callie was too cheap for the hundred dollar valet so she parked up the block in the lot.

"Um, if you ladies don't mind we have a party to attend..." Dominique urged. The girls took a few more pictures and followed her inside.

They were feeling like stars when the DJ announced their entrance. The spotlight found them and escorted them up to the VIP section. They would have preferred to hit the dance floor when the DJ began to play their album.

Jovita and Dominique wouldn't hear of it though since they had invited buyers from record chain stores as well as big box stores. Crucial outlets to push their product to platinum status. The girls were gracious and graceful as they were taken around to smooze and shake hands. Callie kept an eye on the club until she found the eyes she was looking for.

"Excuse me," she said and extricated herself from a conversation with one of the streaming services. She worked her way back down and over to her new friend. "Hey there!"

"Hey yourself!" Ervin greeted back and gave her a hug. "Congratulations!"

"Thank you!" she shouted back between smiles. It didn't

take long before they had enough of yelling over the music. "Let's get out of here!"

"Isn't this your party?" he asked as she pulled him towards the door.

"Yup! It's my party and I can leave if I want to. Leave if I want to..." she sang. They looked both ways when they stepped out onto the busy sidewalk. One way was her adoring fans, so they headed off in the other direction.

"There's a park around the corner," he advised since they were looking for a quiet place to talk instead of screaming at each other over the music.

"I like parks," she smiled and took his hand. They interlocked their fingers and swung their hands as they walked and talked. They found a bench and got comfortable so they could talk some more.

"Who let these rats in here!" Jovita snarled at the ratchet chicks on the dancefloor. They stood out since they were the only ones twerking.

"He did!" Dominique said, twisting her lips at Mike headed towards them. "Where the heck is Callie?"

"Ain't seen her?" Penny replied and looked around again. Zenobia had been right next to her but now she was gone too. "The fuck?"

"Congratulations ladies," Mike offered and clapped his hands as he approached. Dominique saw right through it since she knew him well enough to know he didn't celebrate other people's successes and triumphs.

"Mmhm. What do you want Mike?" she demanded as he looked Jovita up and down like one does their food when the waitress delivers their plates.

"I wouldn't mind a little of that. Shit, both of y'all and we can make it a sandwich," he laughed.

"This is a private party!" Jovita snapped and twisted her face up at the suggested threesome.

"Yeah, but I just wanted to bury the hatchet. Talk a little business," he offered along with his best smile. That smile once allowed him to twist Dominique into all kinds of positions but now she felt nothing. His power was gone.

"Our business is solid. We don't need any help," Jovita huffed and walked off.

"That's an uppity little bitch!" he growled, showing a glimpse of the danger behind the smile. He quickly shook it off and smiled once more. "Let my girls open on your tour? Controversy sells!"

"So does good music. No thanks," she declined and walked off. She didn't feel any of the daggers he shot into her back as she walked off. Not yet anyway.

"Hey!" Zenobia sang happily when she returned to the VIP section. A little too happy and Jovita leaned in to see why.

"Are you drunk?" she reeled, mortified since so many important people were here to see them.

"As a skunk!" she giggled and swayed. It didn't take much since she wasn't much of a drinker plus the pills coursing through her system. It really wasn't a good look with the bigwigs in attendance.

"I'll take her home. Where's Callie?" Dominique asked again but Penny still didn't know.

"I'll take her. Handle our business," she said and escorted Zenobia towards the door. They made it just as Callie made it back inside the club.

"Where y'all going!" she demanded like she wasn't the one who snuck off.

"Where have you been?" Penny asked but got her answer when Ervin came in behind her. "Oooooh!"

"Ooh, nothing. We went to the park to talk," Callie replied. "What's wrong with her?"

"I'm a skunk!" Zenobia sang and cracked up.

"Ooooh!" Callie laughed when it was obvious. She turned to her new friend to cancel breakfast plans but he got it.

"Rain check," Ervin said understandingly. He placed a soft kiss on her cheek and made her blush.

"Awe!" Penny gushed, while Zenobia was a little bolder.

"You ain't finna fuck him?" she wondered why too loudly. "Bruh, give him some pussy! What you saving it for!"

"Ugh!" Callie grunted in embarrassment. "Please excuse my friend. She is a hoe."

"I'ma skunk!" Zenobia repeated as she was taken away.

"Shit!" Penny grunted when she saw the line waiting for the valet.

"Good thing I parked in the lot around the corner," Callie huffed and switched her hips away.

"Cuz you cheap yo!" Penny called behind her. "You rich now ma! Spend some of that bread!"

Callie knew she was on her way to becoming rich but growing up in poverty still affected her. It affects all the newly rich but in different ways. Some become spendthrifts and run through money as fast as they get it. They're the ones holding stacks of cash up to the ear like a phone or dumb shit like spelling dumb shit out on the floor in money.

They brag about fucking up tens of thousands in designer stores while their families are hungry. They spend hundreds of thousands on real jewelry that looks like fake jewelry. Which really defeats the purpose, plus no one cares. They never stop to reflect that the rich jewelers they make richer don't wear any of that shit. The difference between wealth and worth that some will never understand.

"Ah shiiiiiit!" Callie laughed at the thought of wasting her money on frivolous shit. Her mind shot to her numerous shopping sprees but that's where she drew a line. "Clothes don't count!"

"Hey!" someone called as footsteps came up behind her. Callie spun, ready for battle.

"Fuck y'all want?" Callie snapped when she saw the so-called Real Pretty Thugs rushing towards her.

"Smoke!" Jersey Girl shouted and swung on her. Callie dipped the blow and fired off a couple of body shots that doubled her over. She quickly kicked her heels off and took a boxing stance. These girls had no idea she and Voodoo used to play box daily. Plus she grew up in foster care which meant she could fight.

"Come on with it then!" she growled as the other two impostors moved in. Fist and feet flew as loud 'paps' filled the night air. Callie gave as much as she took as she fought the two girls while the third tried to catch her breath. "I can, do this all, day!"

"We not tho," Jersey Girls announced as she came from her blind side. Callie looked just in time to catch the glint of a blade as it sped towards her face. Country Girl and Ki-Ki both went wide eyed and backed away.

"Yeah, y'all hoes better step the fuck off!" Callie popped as her attackers turned and walked off. She felt the burn on her face and got mad. "I know this bitch ain't scratch my face!"

Callie continued on to her car and looked at her reflection in her window. Her head tilted at the smooth line running the length of her cheek. It began to turn white, then gushed with blood. She cupped her face with one hand and jumped behind her wheel. The smell of blood assaulted her nostrils and ruined her dress as she drove. She looked like someone had tossed a bucket of blood in her face by the time she reached Grady hospital.

CHAPTER 14

"How is she?" Dominique asked as she came through the front door.

"She's still a skunk," Penny snickered. She furrowed her brow and twisted her lips when she realized the woman was alone.

"Where's Callie?" Dominique asked before Penny could ask her.

"Being freaky with that guy I bet!" she replied as her phone rang with Callie's face on the screen. "It's her now. Hello?"

"What!" Dominique shrieked when Penny's tanned face went white before she spun and headed out the door. "Where are you going?"

"Grady!" she shouted in the air as she ran down the hall to the elevator. It didn't open when she pounded on the call button so she headed down the stairs. Dominique went to check on Zenobia and found her curled up into the fetal position and snoring loudly.

"Drunk as a skunk!" she laughed and headed back out to check on Callie herself. The tour would net millions of dollars and they didn't need any delays. She was surprised to pull into Grady hospital at the same time Penny did despite the head start. "What took you so long?"

"This!" she fussed and held up the police ticket.

"You got a ticket?" she reeled in disbelief.

"Hell no! I'm too cute!" Penny declared and flipped it over to show the cute cop's phone number. Cute or no cute she balled it up and tossed it over her shoulder because, "Fuck the police!"

"Now you can tell me what's going on!" Dominique demanded as she trailed her inside.

"She ain't say. Just that she was in the emergency room," she said. They reached the information counter and inquired about their loved one.

"Bed eight, but I think the police are still in with her," the woman explained.

"Good timing then!" Dominique declared and marched where the woman pointed. She was in full 'mama bear' mode so Penny let her take the lead. The woman could be totally ferocious when it came to these girls. Even before they were worth millions.

"But, witnesses said you were fighting three girls. How is it possible for you not to have seen their faces?" the lady detective softly goaded.

"Them knuckles sure saw their faces!" her partner

laughed. He had taken Callie's initial claim not to have seen anything, and not knowing who cut her face. He was done with it and ready to move on to the next crime in line.

"Your face!" Penny howled when she saw the fresh, white gauze on Callie's cheek.

"What happened!" Dominique growled and clenched her fist and teeth. Had Callie said it was one of the cops in the room she would have attacked on the spot.

"Ion know," she shrugged and nodded at the cops. The lady cop had especially leaned in to see if she would reveal what they had been trying to pry out of the girl.

"Are y'all done here now?" Dominique asked the police.

"Yes, no," the he and she cops said at the same time.

"Listen, this could have been so much worse. Please have your daughter cooperate with the investigation," the woman said, sounding motherly because she was. Dominique just looked around the room in confusion.

"She's talking to you mommy," Callie cracked and laughed. Only to find out laughing with fresh stitches can be painful. "Owe!"

"Can you guys go now?" Penny asked so politely both Dominique and Callie looked shocked.

"Here's my card. Call me if you change your mind," the woman said and handed the card to the patient.

"Thank you," Callie said and matched her soft smile. Then crumbled it up the second she was gone and tossed it over her shoulder. Because, once again, "Fuck the police."

"Who did this to you?" Dominique repeated.

"You already know," Penny said and shook her head. She

took it extra personally since she shouldn't have let her walk to her car on her own.

"I gave them hoes the business until the ugly one cut me!" Callie bragged.

"They all ugly bruh!" Penny reminded. They shared a laugh and high five as the doctor came in.

"Celebrating?" the young, black man asked with an attitude. He hadn't worked here very long but had seen centuries worth of black on black victims. It just amazed him how people bragged about and posted their war wounds. Some even went live while fighting for their lives.

Have him tell it Black Lives Matter and all those other protests were some bullshit. White cops have no right to kill unarmed black men and that's an undisputed fact. The uproar and outrage was just and justified. However he just pronounced a six month old baby dead from a gunshot, shot by another black person. That baby didn't get a rally, a protest, a speech or nothing.

"No, we just um, dang! You cute!" Penny stammered.

"Thanks," he blurted since the compliment barely registered. He was more worried about the young woman sitting on the bed.

"You need me to take my panties off?" Dominique asked helpfully. That got a smile and blush from the man.

"Maybe later. Right now I need to check these stitches..." he said and peeled the tape holding the gauze.

"Damn!" Penny and Dominique shrieked when they saw the nasty gash running the length of her cheek. Penny pouted and began to sob loudly.

"It's really not as bad as it looks," he assured them and double checked his handiwork. "Luckily her attacker had a very sharp blade."

"Will it leave a scar?" Dominique wanted to know.

"It's all good! Pretty Thug shit!" Callie chanted and held her chin high. She was just as worried about a scar but refused to show it.

"Not much. A thin line at most, she has good skin," he said and pinched her skin to show them what he meant.

"I know a great plastic surgeon in LA! He did all my friends' boobs and noses in high school!" Penny declared. It was followed by a moment of silence for high school girls getting boob and nose jobs.

"You know an excellent plastic surgeon right here in Atlanta," the doctor said and lifted his chin to indicate he was who he spoke of. He fished out his card and handed it to Dominique. "Bring your daughter back in two weeks."

"Yes sir," she said as she accepted it.

"Oh, now I am your daughter huh?" Callie laughed when he left them alone.

"For him you are! Shit I need to get me some doctor dick!" she laughed.

"Paging doctor dick! Doctor dick!" Penny called and cracked up. The Pretty Thugs dodged yet another bullet since this could have been worse. Only cats have nine lives, one of these chicks was going to end up dead.

"The limo is downstairs!" Dominique yelled through the apartment. It was actually still a few minutes out but she knew how long it took these chicks to get out of the mirror. Callie exhaled a deep sigh as she peeled the corner of her bandage off. Something she did daily to check on the healing process.

"Looking better," she said even if it had a way to go. She flexed her face to see if she would actually be able to rap. It was slightly painful but she wasn't going to tell anyone. She smoothed some of the ointment the doctor gave and was set. "I'm coming!"

"I'm coming!" Zenobia called and giggled. Dominique was always rushing them and they learned to shout 'I'm coming' no matter how long it took to actually come. She loaded her personal effects including her new supply of pain pills. The pain of the abortion had long subsided but life was pain and the pills made her feel better.

"I'm ready!" Penny announced as she came from her room. All she carried was a carry-on bag filled with her hygiene items and underclothes. She was dressed casually in an Iqra Ink sweat suit and sneakers. All their clothes for the shows would be provided by their sponsors.

"I called ten minutes ago and y'all still aren't ready?" Jovita asked as she entered the apartment.

"We need a private jet!" Callie proclaimed as she came out with a fresh bandage.

"Are you going to be able to perform?" Jovita asked but couldn't wait for an answer. "Probably not! The first show is tomorrow! This is terrible!"

"I'm good yo!" Callie vowed. She would have to appear with the bandage but the attack only brought more publicity to the group and added to their thug mystique. They rapped about selling weed, shopping and dudes since that's what they lived.

Likewise, the so-called Real Pretty Thugs rap songs about getting drunk, high and fucked. The exact bullshit the masses loved and their album was doing good numbers as well. They were just a few slots behind the Money Dance on the radio.

Of course they were dumb enough to brag about the attack on Callie all over social media. It took a joint effort from Jovita, Dominique and nearly an act of Congress to keep her from clapping back. Their followers and stock went up by the day without it.

"Let's bounce!" Dominique declared after going around to ensure all clothes irons, hair irons and other electronics were all cut off.

"Let's!" Penny cheered and was the first one out of the door.

"Are you excited about going home again?" Jovita asked Penny as she rushed ahead down the hallway.

"As long as the Fire Marshal ain't waiting for her ass," Callie answered for her.

"Ha, ha," she quipped. "Hells yeah! I left in disgrace a year ago and now we got shows booked all up and down the state!"

"And radio, and video, and parties, after parties, photo shoots!" Zenobia added and danced. Her friends smiled happily since they were happy to see her so happy lately. Only because they didn't know it was because she stayed high lately.

"Business class?" Penny winced when she received her boarding pass.

"Still better than flying coach," Callie reminded while Zenobia smiled and sang with the song playing in her ear buds. They took their seats and were all sound asleep before the plane reached cruising altitude. They didn't wake again until they landed.

"Welcome home P-money!" Penny said as they stormed through LAX.

"Dang!" Zenobia exclaimed when she spotted a man holding a sign with their name on it.

"Pretty Thugs, that's us!" Callie added as they made their way over to him. He led them to a limo that took them to their hotel.

"I hope we have the penthouse! It has its own pool!" Penny recalled as they arrived.

"No penthouses this time chica," Dominique replied. The promoters did book them individual rooms but no penthouse. The group was hot but still not the headliners. They would be opening for a superstar called Pretty Boy while their own album climbed the charts.

"I had to pay for our suite out of pocket," Jovita recalled, since that's where she and Dominique would sleep. Once they got checked in she got right down to work. The first show was a day away and then nonstop for months.

"I'll take them for dinner," Dominique decided once she sat her bags down.

"Please!" Jovita laughed. They were too close to success to allow anything to derail them. She was happy she was going along to keep them out of trouble.

CHAPTER 15

"What's in the bag?" Callie dared as they rode over to the radio station. They were booked on the hottest morning show to help promote the show that night.

"Grease," Jovita said and twisted her lips. The way her morals were set up she really didn't like committing crimes. The cash in the bag was payola and that was definitely a crime.

Radio program directors still charged labels cold hard cash to be added to the regular rotation of songs. Which is why people will hear the same song three times just on the drive to work. Dominique had a trick for them though and worked her phone.

"We need a studio!" Dominique announced when she finally rested her phone.

"For?" Jovita asked while the girls took pictures and videos of the scenery.

"S&S, One Ummah and Iqra want us to record commercials using the Money Dance song," she explained. Jovita nodded along and high fived her business acumen.

"So, let them pay to play us nationwide!" Jovita understood. She still had a hundred thousand in cash to spread out to radio and club DJs along the way. When it ran out she would pull another hundred from the bank. It would cost all available cash to launch this record.

"Yup! Then listeners will call in and request the whole song," she concluded.

"Here we are," the driver announced as they reached the station. He put the SUV in park and hopped out to open the doors. A jet black Benz whipped to a stop right in front of them. The booming system vibrated their vehicle as well as the windows of the radio station.

"That's that new Pretty Boy song!" Zenobia cheered on the infectious new song. The doors opened and a puff of smoke billowed out.

"And that's him!" Penny cheered as he hopped out and headed inside. The jet black specimen had a bright, white smile and crop of thick wavy hair. He dripped with diamonds and his signature pearls. Ten thousand dollars worth of mismatched designer clothing and accessories hung haphazardly from his six foot frame. He didn't have a security detail, just his cousin Vinny, with a big gun hanging out of his waistband.

"Because you're opening for him tonight ladies," Jovita informed and set off a round of applause.

"Well let's get inside," Dominique reminded since they were scheduled to go on before Pretty Boy. They filed out and into the building. Of course they were live as they clowned around as they made their way up to the studio.

"Hey! The Pretty Thugs!" a receptionist cheered when she spotted the group. "Macho Man will be with you in a second. Can I get your autographs while you wait?"

"Hey!" they sang and signed autographs while Jovita headed over to the program director's office and tapped on the door.

"Come in!" the woman called and stood. Pretty Boy was just leaving as she came in. He had white powder all over his nose until he wiped it away.

"Hello Ramona. We spoke on the phone," Jovita greeted and shook one hand while she wiggled her nose with the other.

"Have a seat," Ramona sang and sat herself. "Your girls are hot! The phone lines have been blowing up with requests!"

"That's great! So we don't even need this then?" Jovita joked about the envelope of cash in her hand.

"I ain't say all dat!" she laughed and reached for the money.

"Yeah we...." Jovita began but Ramona held up a finger to pause her as she counted the money. A smile spread on her face when she reached the ten grand she charged.

"You were saying?" she asked and tuned in. They spoke business until Macho Man announced his newest guest.

"OK LA! You've been hearing my next guest on all the hottest tracks with the late, greats Lil Bruh and Young Vaughn! P-money and Doobie Daddie are on the top eight at eight. I give you, P-money, Z-money, C-money! Otherwise known as the Pretty Thugs!" he announced.

"Hey LA! Sup yo! Calli love!" they cheered back.

"So, let's cut straight to the chase. Z-money, you were dating Young Vaughn. Reports say you were in the car when he was gunned down..." Macho Man began.

"Oh no!" Dominique groaned. Zenobia had been a zombie for weeks after the shooting. The last thing anyone needed was for anyone to snatch that bandaid off her mental state.

"I thought he agreed not to bring that up?" Jovita asked. They expected questions about Callie getting cut, beef with the fake group, even the first viral video of them coming off stage to fight Gerty and her girls. This was off limits and caught Zenobia off guard.

"He did! That's why they didn't let me in!" she shot back.

"Um, we um..." Zenobia stuttered from the sneak attack. She was on the verge of a panic attack before P-money saved the day.

"How would you feel if your man was shot in front of you? And I know you got a man!" P-money snapped.

"Cuz you a bitch!" C-money added as they both got up. It now made sense why the controversial host was on one side of the large desk while the guest was on the other. It was filled with various and expensive equipment but the Thugs still hopped over all that shit.

"Security!" Macho Man screeched and proved Callie right since he sure sounded like a bitch. The security was present in the room since this wasn't the first time a guest tried to get on his ass. It was the first time they tried to go over the desk instead of around.

"We better get in there!" Jovita shouted and led the charge inside.

"Whoa ladies!" the beefy guards said as they held the tiny girls off their boss. As much as they wanted to see him get his ass whooped, he did sign their checks.

"Callie! Penny!" Dominique called as they struggled to get past the guards. Zenobia began to come out of her funk with a slow giggle like Sophia at the dinner table when Miss Ceily finally snapped at Mister.

"Uh huh, big mouth about to get your ass whipped!" Zenobia laughed at the so-called Macho Man hiding behind his guards.

"Get them out of here!" Macho Man shouted. His guards began to comply but Pretty Boy walked in and shut him down.

"Let em stay," he said smoothly and took a seat next to Zenobia.

"But these bitches..." Macho whined but Pretty Boy raised an eyebrow and shut him down.

"Y'all was about to get on his ass huh," the rap star laughed as Penny and Callie climbed down from the table.

"Can't get in his ass, too crowded!" Callie snapped.

"Told you 'bout that mouth," Pretty Boy shrugged and took over the interview. He asked the same questions fans asked him and let the girls answer. "Play their new song!"

"We, I..." the DJ complained since he, like most DJs have very little control over what they can play. He looked through the window at Ramona who gave him the nod. "You asked for it LA! Here's the debut single from the notorious Pretty Thugs!"

"Catch them opening for me tonight at Staples Arena!" Pretty Boy blurted before the mic was cut off. He and Zenobia shared a glance as she slid by him to leave with her friends. The Petty Thugs had officially turned out the radio station. As with all their previous stunts their adoring fans loved it.

"You see this shit!" Dominique declared when they had thousands of comments on their post about the show.

"Mmhm, and they dragging his punk ass!" Zenobia laughed. She felt somewhat vindicated but still wanted to pop a pill. The fact that she didn't want to take one in front of her family should have been a hint of a problem. People hide their drug use when they know it's a problem.

"This shit is cray-cray!" Penny declared when they arrived at the arena. It was hours before show time but the parking lot was already packed. According to the signs and chants most were there to see Pretty Boy but there were large pockets of Pretty Thug supporters scattered about.

"Get used to it chica. Soon you guys will be headliners!" Dominique assured them. Pretty Boy, like a lot of artists, was ninety percent hype and ten percent talent. One hit song was all it took to become a super star these days. He had a hot album which allowed him to fuel his bad habits. A volatile mix that was bound to catch up to him.

"I'm ready to rip this shit!" Callie growled. She made sure to tag the imitation group so they could see them winning. The fake group was doing small shows in clubs while they were in an arena.

"That's the spirit!" Jovita cheered since that's where she needed them to be. She looked over to Zenobia who was still subdued. "You ready tigress?"

"Rrrr!" she roared and cracked up. She was good and mellow from popping a pill, but ready to go.

"So let's go then!" Penny said and they piled out of the SUV. They would soon get limo service to and from these sold out venues but the tinted out Suburban had to do for now. They did get to use the rear entrance reserved for athletes and stars.

"Dang!" came Zenobia's classic line when they saw the bustling backstage. Until now they had only done clubs and smaller venues. An arena was a whole different ball game. It was Callie's turn next when they saw their name on their very first dressing room.

"This is happening," she practically whispered as they stepped inside. A table was set up with their favorite drinks and snacks for their rider.

It was nothing compared to the riders some artist request. Pretty Boy didn't do a show if there weren't ten bottles of champagne, ten bottles of Henesy, a pound of weed and fried chicken for him and his entourage. The promoters even supplied the cocaine he demanded, it just didn't go on the table. His entourage would run through what they could before the show and keep the rest for the after party.

"Champagne!" Penny cheered of the lone bottle on ice. None of them had asked for it but Jovita knew celebrations were in order.

"Glasses ladies!" she announced and popped the top. They came around and she filled their glasses.

"Ladies, you have an event after the show. A club is paying three thousand dollars just to walk through. Say hello on the mic and take a few pics. Half hour minimum."

"Bruh, someone is paying us three racks for a half hour?" Callie dared and literally twisted her lips dubiously.

"Eight hundred after fees but yeah," Dominique replied.

"Pretty Boy is getting ten grand for that same amount of time. You will too, soon!" Jovita reminded them. There was one stipulation though. "Y'all just have to kill it tonight!"

"Say less!" Penny shot back as she morphed into P-money mode. Her girls transformed too and were ready to body the show.

CHAPTER 16

The Pretty Thugs may have been still an opening act but they still had a big enough movement to place them right before the headliner. A slew of rappers and singers took their turn to woo the massive audience. That audience mostly ignored them since they were here for Pretty Boy as well as the Pretty Thugs. Some of those opening acts were trash, others would someday headline tours of their own.

"You guys are up!" a promoter advised. Dominique had a speech prepared to calm their nerves and hype them up but it wasn't necessary.

"Let's go kill this shit!" Callie snapped and led the charge. Her girls filed in behind her and stomped towards the stage. The opening act who were opening for them only halfway through their song but there was no stopping the Pretty Thugs.

"One sec, you guys..." the promoter was saying as they marched on stage. "Fuck it!"

"Hey!" the hardcore rapper moaned when Callie snatched his mic. He made a move to get it back but P-money shoved him off the stage.

The DJ hadn't cued up their music yet so Callie just took off a capella. The stage hands scrambled to load their back-drops and mics. P and Z monies just leaned in and rapped with Callie on the mic she had stolen from the rapper. He couldn't use it anyway since he broke his arm in the fall. The thousands of fans all rapped along with the group while the DJ finally got their music. He mixed it in at the right moment and it was flawless.

"You see this shit?" Dominique asked in utter amazement. They just made chaos look like it was choreographed. She made sure she was capturing for social media while the film crew did the same from various cameras. Footage that would be pieced together for videos and eventually a documentary.

"These girls are stars!" Jovita said. She was nearly as starstruck as the legions of adoring fans. They watched from side stage as they ran through their album.

"Pretty Boy wants them to stay on stage with him!" Pretty Boy's manager requested as the Thugs wrapped their set.

"Like, dancers?" Dominique asked for clarity. They had just rocked their first arena so she needed to be sure.

"Yeah! That will be dope!" the man cheered at his idea.

"Fuck outa here!" Jovita laughed and shut it down. He

would be dancing for them before she let her girls be extras on anyone's set.

"Yoooo! That was so dope!" Zenobia proclaimed as they cleared the stage. They were all winded and sweaty from giving it all.

"Y'all did that!" Jovita declared and clapped for them as they headed back to their dressing room.

"Now shower and change so we can hit this after party!" Dominique reminded them. There was still money to be made before they went back to the hotel.

"D ang! This piece is packed!" Zenobia exclaimed when they reached the club.

"That's why!" Jovita said, pointing to the sign above.

"Appearing live, Pretty Boy and the Pretty Thugs," Callie read.

"Notice it says, appearing, Not performing," Dominique reminded. The girls were getting paid just to walk through the club. It was a win for the club owner too who could charge more at the door. Then those same people would buy drinks from his bar.

"Let's do this shit so I can sleep!" Callie sighed. Her friends agreed as they headed inside.

"How did he beat us here?" Penny wondered when they saw Pretty Boy and his entourage posted up in the VIP section already.

"He came straight here," Zenobia reasoned, since he was still wearing the same clothes he performed in.

"Well, we have vaginas so..." Penny shrugged. She was right though because sweaty vaginas don't belong in the club. That's why they showered and changed before coming over.

"Facts! I ain't even put no panties on. This thang need to breath!" Zenobia cackled.

"This thang needs some attention!" Callie said. She added a little chucked to make it seem like a joke.

"Too bad ole Savage got killed. We could have taken him on tour with us," Zenobia laughed.

"Suck this dick hoe!" Penny laughed. Jovita just shook her head at their antics while Dominique just lifted her chin. None of them knew she was behind his demise. Nor how close they came from a prison cell instead of a nationwide tour.

"Hmp!" she huffed at the truths she would take to her grave.

"The Pretty Thugs are in the building!" the DJ announced when he got the news. He abruptly cut the Pretty Boy song that was playing and mixed in the Money Dance.

"Hey!!!" Penny declared and switched to P-money mode. Her friends followed suit and followed her to the stage. They did their signature dance until the end of the song. Then joined their managers in the VIP section.

"Y'all hoes make room!" Pretty Boy demanded and cleared the groupies and hangers on from his booth. Once he made room he waved the girls over.

"Mm-mm!" Callie declined and shook her head.

"Don't be like that!" Zenobia declared and led the way over.

"Photo op bae. He has ten million followers," Dominique reminded and steered her over.

"More champagne!" Pretty Boy shouted. He had already stayed longer than he needed but it was clear he wasn't going anywhere.

"No thanks," Jovita declined but she was the only one. Dominique accepted a glass but only to be polite. She actually passed it off to one of the groupies still hovering around on her way to collect their fee.

"Don't be no skunk..." Penny reminded in Zenobia's ear. Since the girl couldn't hold her liquor.

"I'm good!" she shot back and tossed the drink down her throat to prove it.

"Y'all did y'all thing!" Pretty Boy congratulated as he reached under the table to grip Zenobia's thigh.

"You did too!" Callie cheered even though she didn't see the set. Only because she didn't like him or his misogynistic music. He had little respect for women and was a champion for drug abuse.

"Mmmm," Zenobia hummed and spread her legs a little.

"A'ight now!" the rapper reeled when she soaked his fingers instantly. She spread them just a little wider so he could slide a finger inside. He dipped it and pulled it out for a taste. "Damn girl! That thang sweet!"

"Mmhm," she said and knocked down another glass. "Get you a sip!"

"Well ladies, we have a full day tomorrow," Jovita announced when Dominique returned. Everyone stood except Zenobia.

"Y'all go 'head," she said and held her glass out for another refill.

"You bugging yo!" Callie protested and was done with it. Zenobia was grown and was free to do whatever she wanted to do. She stated her position and turned to leave while Penny sat back down.

"I'm staying too," she declared and got a nod of approval from Dominique. Callie shook her head the whole way out the door.

"Let's ride!" Pretty Boy announced and led the large exodus toward the door. He took Zenobia under his arm with Penny by her side. His squad of homeboys and security followed behind with the groupies following them.

"You can ride with me," Cousin Vinny told Penny as they headed out to the valet. She began to decline until the Bugatti pulled up.

"Unless you wanna sit on my lap!" Zenobia laughed as she sat down and treated the world to a nice crotch shot.

"Eww, no!" she shot back at both. A four door Mercedes pulled up next and Penny climbed in the passenger seat. Vinny couldn't keep up with the super car since it had a much larger engine and a coke-head behind the wheel.

"So..." Vinny began as he looked down at the thick thighs on the passenger seat.

"Nope!" Penny shot back to shut down whatever he had

on his mind. It wasn't hard to guess what that was since his eyes stayed on her legs. "Uh, red light..."

"Shit!" he said as he blew through the red light.

"Let me see that thang again..." Pretty Boy said as he reached back between Zenobia's legs. She made it easy on them both and put a foot on the dash.

"Don't get mad when I, ssss, cum all over your leather seats!" Zenobia warned as he worked his fingers.

"Don't threaten me with a good time!" he laughed and kept doing what he was doing. They made it to the hotel before she could keep her word so he rushed her inside and up to his suite. Vinny violated a few more traffic laws so he could keep up with his cousin. Pretty Boy paid the bills so he couldn't let anything happen to him. Luckily they made it through unscathed and pulled into the hotel.

"This is nice!" Zenobia sang as they entered the penthouse suite. It wouldn't be long before promoters had to book penthouses for them as well.

"Come on..." he said since he didn't have time for a tour. He pulled her into the bedroom and pulled off his clothes. She nodded in approval when his dick dangled between his legs. It had a nice length and thickness, even soft.

"You got condoms?" she needed to know, because she was not going through another abortion.

"Hell yeah!" he said excitedly even if he didn't need it right away. He laid her back on the bed and dipped face first under her dress.

"Oh, OK then!" she said when he licked her labia like a lollipop. Once again she made it easier by kicking her legs wide and high. Zenobia heard the party in the living room when the rest of the guests arrived. Pretty Boy stopped abruptly and reached for his pants. "What's wrong?"

"Break time!" he announced and dumped a pile of cocaine on her hard stomach. She leaned forward and watched as he sifted it around with his finger. Then leaned in and inhaled a pile each nostril. He grimaced as the raw coke reached its destination, then saw her looking down at him. "My bad. Have some?"

"No. Yes. What does it do? Un-uh," she vacillated. In the end that same curiosity that killed that cat that time, came into play. "Just a lil..."

"A'ight," Pretty Boy said and scooped some from the package with a fingernail grown especially for scooping cocaine from the package. Except he was a whole coke-head and had no concept of 'a lil' so he scooped a lot and held it up to her nostrils. "Sniff!"

"Argh!" Zenobia grunted when the pure coke burned her nose.

"Come on, one more. So you don't be lopsided," he said and scooped another scoop.

"Un-uh! It burns! I..." she protested but the intense euphoria that is cocaine changed her mind. He presented the hit and she quickly sucked it up her nostril. She laid back to enjoy the buzz and spread her legs once again.

"Pretty Thug got a pretty pussy!" Pretty Boy declared as he leaned back in for desert. Zenobia didn't stand a chance between the pure coke and the whirlwind tongue.

"Damn nigga!" she shouted as she had the strongest

orgasm of her life. She shivered and shook for a moment but was ready for some dick once she recovered. "Fuck me!"

"Huh?" Pretty Boy asked even though it wasn't his hearing that wasn't working. Zenobia refused to be the first woman in history to have to tell a man twice to fuck her. She took matters into her own hands and reached down for the dick. She was so high and so horny she almost forgot about a condom.

"Ewww! What's wrong!" she reeled and snatched her hand away from the flaccid dick.

"Shit, I done snorted too much coke," he explained, then reached for the package to snort some more.

"So, you can't fuck?" she wondered since this was new for her.

"You may have to suck on it for a sec," he underestimated. She could have sucked on it for an hour and it wasn't going anywhere. Especially since he kept on snorting more coke.

"OK, except hell naw!" Zenobia laughed. She let out a sigh at not getting fucked but sat up for the consolation prize. "Let me get some more."

"Hmmmmm!" Penny groaned in the front room. She was only here to watch out for her friend but the groupies kept asking questions and trying to talk to her. When she got tired of talking she pulled out her phone and checked her social status. Her post and pics had tens of thousands of likes and comments which meant more money in the bank.

"Come here," Cousin Vinny ordered one of the groupies. She jumped up and hopped over the coffee table to answer the summons. He leaned back and pulled his dick out when she sat beside him. The groupie knew just what to do so she dropped her head on his lap and inhaled the dick. Penny had seen enough and stood.

"Yo, Z! Time to go! Now!" she demanded and banged on the bedroom door. She paused for a second and pushed the door open.

"Come on in!" Pretty Boy cheered but Zenobia scrambled off the bed.

"I'm coming!" she said and rushed for the door. Pretty Boy got off the bed and Penny watched his dick swing as he came out behind them completely naked.

"Say Vinny, drop them off," he ordered.

"A'ight," Vinny agreed and took his dick back. He hopped up and led the way out to carry out the demand.

"You, come on," Pretty Boy told the same groupie whose mouth his cousin just vacated.

"What?" Zenobia asked when she saw Penny looking at her. Guilt told her it was her nose so she wiped it to make sure there was no residue left.

"Nothing man," Penny sighed. She was a rich white girl so she knew all the signs of cocaine use.

CHAPTER 17

"Vegas!" Callie cheered as the plane began its descent into Sin city. They had toured all over California for the last week but now it was time to move on.

"Dang!" Penny exclaimed when they saw the city from above. She had to borrow Zenobia's word since she had taken a private jet with Pretty Boy and his entourage. They spent quite a bit of time together in California but still hadn't had sex. Only because the rapper spent his life high off cocaine and couldn't get his dick hard.

Zenobia still popped her pills but was enjoying her new found friend, cocaine. She enjoyed the push and pull of the contradictory drugs. She could sleep, eat and felt great. Even if the combination of drugs killed more people than Desert Storm in Iraq. She didn't mind watching the groupies suck on the rappers dead dick while she drank, smoked and snorted coke. Penny and Callie didn't like her new friends but she politely reminded them that she was grown. They were all twenty one now and had no parents to tell them what to do.

"You think that's something, look at this!" Jovita proudly proclaimed and showed the sales records on her laptop.

"Nuh-uh!" Dominique dared. She expected these numbers, just not this quick.

"Un-uh! Platinum in two damn weeks!" Jovita screamed. All eyes in the business class section turned in their direction to see the celebration. The stewardess didn't mind since it was nothing compared to the chaos back in coach.

"Wow!" Callie said when she looked at the other name on the screen. Young Vaughn had just gone double platinum even though he wasn't around to promote his project. The Pretty Thugs paid homage to him by letting his song play at each set.

"But wait, there's more!" Jovita announced like an infomercial. The good news tinged with bad news just as quickly subdued her. Dominique already knew so she jumped in and helped out.

"You guys got your advances," she said and left out the part about Young Vaughn's insurance payout. Both Penny and Callie scrambled to check their accounts on their phones. The recent deposit of eight hundred grand pushed their six figure accounts into the next tax bracket.

"Bruh, I'ma millionaire!" Callie cheered. Penny was stoic at the milestone. She wouldn't be satisfied until she reached a billion.

An SUV awaited the girls arrival and whisked them to the hotel and casino the promoter booked their rooms. Once they put their bags down they met down in the restaurant. They were joined before the waitress could take their order.

"Well, hello there miss! Glad you could join us!" Jovita sang, somewhat sarcastically.

"Hey y'all! How I got a million dollars in my account?" Zenobia wanted to know.

"The advance Ethan promised us!" Penny proudly proclaimed.

"Dang!" she said and took a seat. That first million is heavy like that and makes a person have a seat. Plus she was starving. "I want a big ass steak!"

"They bugging with these prices though!" Callie fussed and grimaced.

"Uh girlfriend, we're rich!" Zenobia reminded and waved her hand for a waitress.

"We kinda are," Penny agreed. She had already made her selections by the time the waitress made it over. "Surf and turf. Wagyu."

"A5?" the lady asked since she made a commission on the five hundred dollar steaks.

"But of course!" she shot back like what else. Zenobia ordered the same while Callie settled for a fifty dollar cheese burger and fries.

"Champagne too!" Zenobia ordered since they were celebrating. "Y'all excuse me..."

There was a moment of silence while her friends tried to ignore the changes in the girl. She seemed so different, so quickly. Part was the drugs but the fame was just as bad. In fact, fame is the worst drug known to man. *It's stronger than* heroin. When you can look in the mirror, like there I am, and still not see what you become. (Jay-Z).

Callie and Penny were changing as well, just not as drastically. It was inevitable and infectious. A literal avalanche of money and fame was speeding towards them. If they weren't careful, very careful they would be completely buried.

"Well, we have a whole night to ourselves before the show..." Penny offered suggestively even though she knew exactly how she wanted to do.

"Ooh, I know! Can we check out the casino?" Dominique dared and laughed.

"Pretty Boy 'ndem already down there," Zenobia relayed and looked herself over in the tiny dress she had selected for the night.

"I guess I can try the slot machines?" Callie guessed. It looked like fun even if she wasn't particularly partial to gambling. She was still mad about Voodoo for losing a few thousand dollars playing C-lo.

"I have calls to make. I'll come down when I'm finished," Jovita said. Dominique led the girls down to the casino even if she couldn't keep up with them all. Especially from the blackjack table.

"I guess I can stand a grand?" Dominique announced when they reached the bank of ATM machines. The branch was actually open twenty hours a day to help separate fools from their money. She hoped to set the standard at a thousand dollars.

'sheeeeeet' Callie thought to herself and laughed at the idea of just giving away a thousand dollars. She would one day make that much in a few minutes but she wouldn't just give it away then either. She inserted her ATM card and vacillated on the preset options. In the end 200 sounded better than 500 and she agreed. The twenties would be swapped out for one dollars bills to feed the one arm bandits known as slot machines.

"Or five..." Penny decided and pulled five thousand from the machine.

"For real, for real," Zenobia agreed and pulled five thousand as well. She heard Pretty Boy and company before she saw them crowded around the dice table.

"I'll be at the poker table," Penny announced and took off. Dominique headed over to the roulette table to bet on black.

"There she is!" Pretty Boy cheered when he spotted Zenobia headed towards them. The groupies by his side instinctively spread out to make room before Cousin Vinny had to move them.

"Hey," she sang and turned her cheek when he leaned in to kiss her. She didn't mind licking her own vagina juice off his thick lips in private but no kissing in public. There was something else she liked to do in private so she leaned in and asked, "You got some powder?"

"Girl you know I do!" he said and slipped her a vial of coke. "Blow on these 'fo you go!"

'Phew!' she huffed on the dice and headed off to powder

her nose. She heard the entourage erupt behind her when the dice landed on seven.

"See what we got here..." Zenobia said once she entered the stall. The custom vial was designed exclusively for snorting drugs since the top had a little spoon built in. She used it to take two scoops up each nostril to go with the opiates already in her system. She walked, wiping her nose and straight into a familiar face. "Oh hey!"

"Hey hell!" Callie fussed. She grew up in Harlem, New York and knew a coke user when she saw one. She ignored the obvious signs but this was right in her face. "What are you doing Z!"

"Partying! Chill! I got this!" she assured her and headed back out to her party.

"Don't let it get you ma," Callie sighed and did what she came to do. Then went back to pulling slot machines with the old ladies.

"Here comes my good luck charm!" Pretty Boy announced when Zenobia returned. The roll she blew on hit for ten grand. He had lost thirty grand in her brief absence. "Blow babe!"

'Phew' she blew, and he promptly rolled another winner.

"Oh hell naw!" Cousin Vinny shouted and began betting with them against the house. Zenobia joined in and flipped her own five grand into sixty. She was bit by the gambling bug and picked up another bad habit by the time they called it a night.

"Send ten bottles of Moèt and five bottles of Henny up to

the suite," Pretty Boy ordered as he took Zenobia under his arm.

"I ain't finna drank nothing else!" she declared and wobbled in her heels. She was good and drunk on top of the other drugs circulating through her system.

"You might.." he laughed as she got heavier in his arm. He would be practically carrying her by the time they reached the penthouse.

"You want me to take her to her room?" Vinny offered. It wasn't chivalry either since he was a savage.

"And let this go to waste!" Pretty Boy laughed since he was a savage too. He took Zenobia into his room and spread her out on the bed. Her legs spread next and he dove tongue first into her twat.

Zenobia had literally passed out from the drug interaction and didn't get to enjoy the tongue play. Pretty Boy tugged at his dick but it was too numb from snorting coke. He rubbed it against her pussy lips but that didn't help. Even when he pushed it into her open mouth it didn't respond. Eventually he gave up and headed back out for more coke.

"Want me to drive you?" Cousin Vinny offered since it was his job. It was also his duty as family to keep him safe even though he often snuck away to do things he didn't want anyone knowing.

"Nah," Pretty Boy said over his shoulder as he headed out.

"Sheeeet..." Vinny said as he hopped up. He didn't know if he would be gone for a long or little so he had to hurry.

Unlike his cousin he had no problem getting an erection.

Especially when he saw Zenobia completely naked on the bed. He wished he had time to strip and join her but Pretty Boy could return at any moment. Plus the group of groupies and hangers on in the next room.

He dropped his draws and climbed on top of the inebriated young woman. She wouldn't get to enjoy him sucking her nipples so he did it for his own sake. Then rubbed his erection against her vagina. She was still wet from the slobber and saliva left behind which helped him ease inside.

"Damn shawty!" he gushed when her tight box gripped like a vice. She didn't get to enjoy the compliment but he didn't get to enjoy that tight pussy for very long. A few slow humps was all it took to bust a nut. It was bad enough he was inside of her without permission but busting a nut in her was even worse. He didn't bother washing his dick as he scrambled to get out of her and the room before his cousin made it back.

"Sup," Pretty Boy said as he came back into the suite. He ignored the replies as he headed back into his room. He stripped, ate the pussy one more time and began smoking the coke he copped while he was out.

CHAPTER 18

"Mmhm..." Callie challenged when Zenobia came in. She wanted to fuss her out about last night but the look on her face put that on pause. "What's wrong?"

"Ion know?" she replied she had to wonder for herself. Not only did she feel weird from the drugs but she was sore between her legs and didn't remember having sex. She awoke to Pretty Boy snorting coke and watching porn so she knew he didn't fuck her. Someone did, though and she was sure. She hadn't been with anyone since Vaughn died and knew she had been recently penetrated.

"Cuz you partying too hard ma!" Callie warned as Penny came from the bathroom.

"Slow down chica!" she huffed as well since they had agreed to confront their friend about her partying. She saw the look on her face as well and switched gears. "You OK?"

"Huh? Yeah. Hell yeah! Ready to turn this show out tonight!" she proclaimed and got hyped. Meanwhile, the tug of her budding addictions nagged at her. She had some pills in her bag but could use a bump cocaine provides. Plus she romanced the rolling dice at the crap table.

"Yo? You good?" Callie laughed as she watched the girl drift into her head.

"Huh? Oh, mmhm. What y'all tryna do today?" Zenobia shot back to switch the focus from her.

"Shopping!" Penny shouted back, to no one's surprise. Vegas was a high roller city with tons of high end shops and her bank account was filling faster than she could spend. Managers don't eat unless their clients eat so Jovita and Dominique hunt for deals and checks like sharks hunt for food.

"I'm tryna smash some of this food!" Callie said. She had been watching Food Paradise Vegas and wanted to try them all.

"I was thinking about going back to the casino? I had fun! I won, like, fifty racks!" Zenobia stated. She left out the part about losing it back as well the initial five thousand she withdrew. It was nothing compared to the hundred grand Pretty Boy left at the crap table. He easily shrugged it off since he made that much every day of his life.

Still, it was the thrill of the roll that had Zenobia in it's clutches. Watching the dice tumble down the felt knowing you won or lost when they came to a stop. It was just another drug for her to become addicted to. She decided she had sworn off the cocaine when she awoke that morning but by the time they finished brunch she was longing for a hit, or two.

"Hello ladies!" Jovita cheered as she and Dominique arrived at their table.

"Hey!" they sang like a singing group.

"You guys ready for the show?" Dominique asked and picked up a menu.

"Uh, no. We got twelve hours until showtime," Penny quipped.

"True that. So, what's on the agenda for the day?" Dominique asked.

"Shopping! Eating! Casino!" the group shot back like solo artists.

"Pick one because there will be a camera crew with you guys today," Jovita announced.

"Shopping! Eating! Casino!" the group shot back once again. Their managers both shook their hands and laughed.

"Well, you guys can do all of that. Just do it together," Dominique directed.

"A day in the life of Pretty Thugs..." Jovita said dramatically. They shared a good laugh but that was the agenda.

"Well, I need to holla at Tony before I go. I left my chain up there," Zenobia announced as they headed back to their rooms to change clothes once again.

"Tony?" Callie asked.

"Yeah, that's Pretty Boy's name. I ain't finna call no nigga no damn pretty nothing!" she laughed. Penny and Callie laughed along with her then got off on their floor while she continued up to the penthouse. Timing was everything since Pretty Boy had just awakened from a rare bout of sleep.

"Shit!" Pretty Boy fussed when he awoke. He had a nice

rock hard, morning erection but Zenobia wasn't next to him. They had been hanging out for weeks and he still hadn't been able to fuck her since he couldn't get it up. Now he was so hard his dick throbbed and she was nowhere to be found. Still, he had to fuck something so he rushed out into the living area where the groupies were strewn about.

"Sup cuz?" Cousin Vinny asked when the boss rushed out urgently. He just ignored the raging erection sticking out.

"Tryna fuck something..." he said, looking at the women laid out from a long night of drugging and drinking. A Latina chick lifted her head when she heard voices and got picked. "You! Come!"

"Nice selection," Cousin Vinny laughed since he already fucked her too. Pretty Boy stayed to high so his cousin fucked most of the groupies. Whether they consented or both, whether they were awake or not, Including the one who just rang the bell. He pulled the door open and came face to face with Zenobia. "Oh, hey."

"He up?" she asked and started towards the bedroom.

"Yeah but..." Vinny was saying but she pulled the door open and saw the rest of his answer. She froze for a second to register Pretty Boy having unprotected sex with the stranger. He didn't even notice before she pushed the door back closed. She didn't care since she wasn't into him like that, nor was she really here for him or any chain.

"You got coke?" she asked when she turned back around.

"I got coke," he confirmed since that was one of his duties. He refused to cop the crack rocks his cousin was smoking lately since crack was a downhill ride like a winter Olympic slalom.

"Well give me some!" she fussed like a boss.

"Coming up," he laughed, but only because the joke was on him since he fucked her in her sleep. It more than covered the few grams of coke he took from a larger cache. Zenobia wasted no time and took a few scoops up each nostril right there on the spot.

"Mmmm!" Zenobia moaned as the drug quickly coursed through her system. Now she was ready to start her day.

"Oh my!" Callie cheered as she admired a pair of boots. She adored them but that brand wasn't paying her so she moved on to the one that was. "OK this is it!"

"Nice!" Zenobia sang. She had sponsors too so she plucked a pair of Iqra Ink's sandals to fawn over. "Winner!"

"Ooh! I have to have a pair as well!" Penny added.

"Got it!" the camera announced to their joint relief. He had enough footage of their shopping spree to edit into a nice clip.

"Good, can we eat now!" Callie fussed. She had racks and racks of free clothes that she got paid to wear so she didn't particularly care for shopping. She did like to eat though and Vegas is a foodie town.

"Yes please!" Zenobia sighed since she was ready to go gamble.

"Yeah, let's eat," Jovita agreed. That too was business since she had arranged a meet and greet at a celebrity burger joint.

They headed over to the next event to be filmed and photographed while they ate and smoozed it up. Callie was even allowed into the kitchen to cook her own burger. The result was dubbed the 'C-money burger' and added to the menu. Had she been Jovita's client she would have worked out a royalty for every burger sold.

Zenobia only picked over her food since the hits of coke she snuck in every bathroom visit had robbed her appetite. Luckily she had a nice breakfast since she planned to run through the rest of the coke before the day was out.

'Final-fucking-my!' Zenobia thought when they made it back to the hotel. They headed up to their room to change since there would be more filming. She made sure to wear her sponsor's clothing since it would make up for the ten thousand dollars she pulled from her account.

Callie twisted her lips when she saw Zenobia pulling more money since claimed to have won thousands the night before. She shrugged it off since it wasn't her money or business. Then headed back over to the slot machines to pull the handle a few hundred times. A camera followed each of them to their prospective spots and got more footage until show time.

"You're bluffing?" a professional player dared from across the poker table.

"Gonna cost you another rack to find out," Penny

shrugged and pushed two five hundred dollar chips into the pot.

"I call you and your bluff!" he shot back and matched the bet. He refused to be outplayed by an amateur. He flipped his cards and announced, "Straight flush!"

"Dang!" Penny whined, wide eyed. The crowd 'oohed' and 'aahed' to add to the drama as she flipped her hand.

"Royal flush!" the dealer announced as Penny reached for her winings. The professional poker player had enough and stormed off. Penny was stacking her chips when she felt a tap on her shoulder. She took a sip of her soda before turning around to the face that made her choke.

"Don't choke dear!" the woman offered and patted her back.

"The fuck are you doing here Misty?" Penny managed through the coughs.

"You know this is one of my favorite spots! Your dad used to take me all the time!" Misty reminded, which reminded her that this was where her father was killed.

"I, I mean you, he..." Penny stammered at a rare loss for words. She looked at Misty, the camera then at the other familiar face on the man who walked up behind Misty.

"Ready babe?" the judge who ruled in her favor asked as he wrapped his hands around her waist.

'Oh no!' Callie screamed in her mind when she saw the look in her friend's eye. She rushed over to save the day since they had a show in a few hours. It was too late when life shifted to slow motion and Penny switched to P-money.

"Bitch..." P-money grunted and socked Misty in her

mouth. It was an explosion of botox and lip gloss when she connected. Misty reeled back a few steps that knocked the old judge on his old ass. Misty stayed on her feet and smiled through her bloody lips.

"This is what I've been waiting on!" Misty declared and put up her hands. P-money may have been a lunatic but Misty was trailer trash and knew how to fight. She launched a quick attack that would have been ugly for the Pretty Thug if C-money hadn't arrived.

This situation was beyond talking so she jumped into the fray and rocked Misty upside her head. Misty was no punk though and fought the two gallantly. Until another Pretty Thug came flying over the poker table. This one was coked up too so Misty was in trouble.

"The fuck is wrong with you!" Dominique snapped at the security guard. Instead of guarding security he was filming the action.

"My bad," the man said and moved in. It was three against one so he snatched the one away from the onslaught of fists and nails.

"Shit!" Jovita fussed at the scene. Her idea to film the girls had just backfired. Even if she had confiscated the footage from the film crew it was still captured by cell phones from every angle. Not to mention hotel security cameras and now body cam from the police who showed up.

"I want her arrested!" Misty declared, pointing at Penny, Only because she was the only one left. Callie was from Harlem and knew to flee a crime scene before the cops came.

Zenobia had cocaine in her pocket so she didn't stick around either.

"Man!" Penny fussed as she was cuffed behind her back.

"Don't say shit! We're right behind you!" Dominique called after her. Jovita was a boss in business but this was some good shit. Right up Dominique's alley.

CHAPTER 19

"Penelope Manning please," Dominique asked politely when she arrived at the police station. She had the company's black card to pay whatever on the bail. It had taken hours just to be processed into the busy station and the opening acts would soon be on the stage.

"Let's see here..." the intake officer said as he typed in the name. "Penelope Manning, two counts of battery. Elderly abuse since one victim was over sixty five..."

"Excuse me officer," a passerby intervened. "Did you say, Penelope Manning?"

"Yeah sarge. Assaulted a Misty Manning. Wonder if they're related?" the cop answered and asked. The man spun on his heels without answering since he had some questions of his own to ask.

"Who was that?" Dominique needed to know since he took such an intense interest in her girl.

"Homicide detective," he replied and the plot thickened.

"Excuse me. Penelope Manning, do you remember me?" the detective asked when he entered the interview room Penny was being held in. Her celebrity status spared her from the holding cell filled with women of different demographics. It was too hot, too crowded and smelled like a fish pussy on a period.

"Yeah, when my dad died?" she recalled the face but not the name.

"Right. Detective Ricker. I worked in the robbery division then but have since moved to homicide," which explained why he had the case twice.

"Misty and Greg killed my dad. Case closed!" she shot back and tensed for the fight that didn't come.

"Yeah, I know," he acknowledged and nodded. "I just can't prove it. Greg died of a fentanyl overdose before I could arrest him. He would have flipped on Misty but without him..."

"You can't do nothing," Penny said and twisted her lips.

"Maybe not, but I won't stop trying," he offered, sincerely enough to be believed. "What I will do is get these charges dropped. She certainly needed her butt kicked!"

"She needs her ass killed!" Penny growled as he left the room. He pretended not to hear it since she was correct. The detective pulled some strings and called in some favors and Penny was cut loose.

"Hey girl! You good?" Dominique asked when Penny emerged from the belly of the precinct. Penny replied by slamming into her and sobbing loudly. All Dominique could do was hold her and rock her until she got it all out. "You good chica. Let it out."

"I'm good," Penny announced a full few minutes later. It wasn't until anger pushed the sorrow away that she could recover. Dominique's phone buzzed incessantly but she had more pressing matters than being late for the show.

"Good, cuz you need to be on stage in a few minutes!" Dominique advised and pulled her towards the exit. The flash of cameras nearly blinded them as they stepped out into the media frenzy. Videos from the casino went viral so a plethora of paparazzi were here to capture her being released.

"How's about an escort?" Detective Ricker asked and led the women over to his own car. He turned on his lights and sirens and sped over to the venue.

"The fuck she at!" Callie griped when Penny's phone went straight to voicemail once more. In all the commotion she never turned it on after getting her property back from the cops.

She looked around the dressing room when she didn't get an answer and saw she was alone. Zenobia had dipped back into the bathroom to powder the inside of her nose once again. Jovita tried Dominique once again just as the promoter burst into the dressing room.

"What the heck is going on! Is she here yet?" he demanded frantically. Not only was his opening act all over the news the main act hadn't arrived yet either. Pretty Boy wasn't in his dressing room and wasn't answering calls.

"OK, what if I was undressed tho!" Callie shot back at the intrusion.

"Nothing I ain't seen! Now where is the rest of the group? You're supposed to be on now!" he moaned.

"She's here!" Jovita cheered when she took Dominique's call just as Zenobia emerged from the bathroom. She was powered up and ready to go.

"Well, let's go tear this shit up then!" she growled and led the march from the room. Callie fell instep behind her on the way to the stage.

"Look, I may need your girls to do a few extra songs. I can't find our headliner," he moaned. If he was looking for sympathy he wouldn't find it here. Jovita was a business woman and her business was music.

"Sure! We got you!" she cheered and waited for his face to light up before giving him the rest. "Just cut another check for twenty thousand and they will do their whole album!"

"I, we, I mean they..." he stammered and checked his phone. None of the calls or messages were from Pretty Boy's camp so he had no choice. "Done!"

Meanwhile, two thirds of the Pretty Thugs took the stage and went to work. It was a gamble since Penny had just arrived at the venue. Jovita worked her magic and Penny was given a mic as soon as she stepped inside. The detective gathered more cops and pushed through the crowd just as her part in the song came up.

P-money rapped and dapped her way through the crowd, surrounded by a police escort and was a sight to be seen. All eyes were on her already from the drama at the casino but this entrance was extra, even for her. This was superstar status. The crowd lifted her onto the stage while still rapping. She broke into their signature Money Dance and they went crazy.

"Keep going! Whole album!" Jovita shouted from side stage, after informing the DJ. They would find out about the extra money later but gladly stayed on stage.

"Hey!" the promoter cheered and let out a sigh of relief when Cousin Vinny appeared backstage. "Thank God!"

"Yeah, no. He's not here," he sighed. Pretty Boy had snuck off earlier and hadn't been heard from since. His phone was off and he wasn't thinking about checking voicemails.

"Where the hell is he?" the man pleaded.

"Good question?" Vinny asked in reply. He had checked all the crack spots and dealers he knew in town. No one had seen him since he was cooped up in a shady motel with a couple ounces of crack and a crackhead. That was a wrap for the rapper for the night.

Not that he was missed since the Pretty Thugs stole the show anyway. There were a few boos when it was announced that he wasn't appearing but they kept right on performing. Even rapping their new lyrics over classic hip hop beats. Superstar status indeed.

The Pretty Tour continued throughout the southwest, then up to the Midwest. Pretty Boy was a no show in St Louis but showed up in Kansas city. He missed Detroit but turned it out in Milwaukee. The promoter paid the group extra to headline but everyone was happy when he showed up to the next city. Especially Zenobia since he brought a boatload of coke with him. She had to get by on just pills alone for days and it upset her balance.

"They said Pretty Boy checked in..." Callie laid out and squinted so she wouldn't miss her reaction.

"So," Zenobia shrugged and kept on scrolling. The infatuation for him had waned but she did like his drugs. As well as the party that raged around him at all times.

"So, you not going up there to hang out?" Callie dared. Penny even stopped scrolling and looked up to see the answer.

"I might. Only cuz I'm grown tho!" she snapped and stood. Now she had a good reason to storm out and head up to the penthouse. "Like I'ma damn child..."

"Mmhm," Callie laughed at the predictable outcome.

"She's good. We good!" Penny reminded, then got up to answer the knock on the door.

"Ladies..." Jovita greeted as she and Dominique entered. "Where's Z?"

"Where else?" Callie quipped.

"We can fill her in later," Jovita sighed and got down to

business. They had plenty of good news to share but Dominique couldn't wait.

"The album is double platinum! Plus, the streaming is through the roof!" she shared excitedly.

"Plus, more brands are lining up!" Jovita added and turned on her laptop. Penny and Callie squinted at the image, turned to each and cracked up at the Pretty Thug dolls. They only vaguely resembled the girls but it was them.

"Is that for real!" Callie demanded through her chuckles.

"Can't be!" Penny guffawed and slapped her knee.

"They offered four million dollars for the rights," Dominique announced and made them choke on their laughter.

"Shoot, I almost signed the deal for you guys!" Jovita cracked up.

"You should have!" they both shouted.

"We got another offer for your official merchandise," Dominique added and paused to bait them up.

"For how much?" Penny fussed with a hand on her hip.

"Two million. I turned it down," she replied.

"It's worth twenty times that," Jovita added. They had their merchandise printed up and sent ahead to each stop on the tour. Sometimes they sold out before the show even came to town.

"This is crazy..." Callie marveled once more. Coming from where she came from it was still hard to believe where she was or where she was going.

"And it's only just beginning!" Dominique reminded. They weren't even halfway through the tour but generated a couple million dollars. It was just the beginning but it wouldn't all be good.

"Yeah, there is a bit of bad news?" Jovita continued and looked over to Dominique.

"Not necessarily bad. I wouldn't say bad," she guessed. They went back and forth while the girls followed like a tennis match.

"Oooh! I know!" Callie cheered and raised her hand like a nerdy student who knows the answer. "How about just telling us?"

"And we'll determine how we feel about it," Penny finished.

"I'll just play it," Dominique decided and pulled up her media player. The Thugs both grimaced at the wack beat that began to play. Their heads began to shake to decline using this track on the next album.

"Ion like it! Nuh-uh!" they agreed.

"No it's not for you guys..." Jovita said just as the rapping began. Penny and Callie began to laugh since they recognized the knockoff Pretty Thugs. The lyrics were even worse since they didn't have Lil Bruh to write for them anymore. Their laughter came to an abrupt end when they registered what they were actually saying.

'*C-money is doo- doo. Bitch I'll do you like they did Voodoo...*'

"Wait, did she say Voodoo's name?" Callie asked and tilted her head in confusion.

"Yeah, it's a diss track," Jovita replied and Dominique stopped the music.

"Un-uh, let it play!" Penny demanded. She complied and let the music play. Next up was White girl Ki-ki talking about P-money, her father and other personal attacks. Next up was Country Girl talking bad about Zenobia, her mother, father and brother. Nothing was off limits in the scathing dis track.

"This is out?" Penny practically croaked.

"Never mind that! I wanna know how these hoes know all our personal shit!" Callie snapped at Dominique.

"Mike! Who else!" Dominique shot back. "Child I would never share anything you girls told me! Obviously they could say a lot more if I did!"

Callie nodded in the veracity. She had shared far more secrets with her mentor than was on the track. They all had but Dominique wasn't the source.

"It hasn't been released yet. The engineer gave me a copy," Jovita said just above a whisper since leaks like that are pretty serious. He was just loyal to Ethan and had to warn them. It was for their second album so there was time to do something.

"I'm going to talk to Mike. I'll offer to drop the cease and desist if they don't release the track," Dominique offered.

"And let them hoes keep eating off our hustle? Fuck naw!" Callie snapped. Her hand instinctively went up to the thin line left of her face from getting cut.

"They ain't making no noise! A flash in the pan," Jovita said and she was right. The public loved the drama and beef but the hype was dying down since their music couldn't stand on it's own. They needed the beef to fuel their careers.

"Man, fuck them ugly bitches!" Penny decided and was done with it. Her bank account had doubled since they left on tour. It would double again before they returned to Atlanta. Then record their second album and double that. More endorsement deals, more features, more money, and more problems.

CHAPTER 20

"Set out another ounce!" Pretty Boy demanded as they flew private to Chicago. Zenobia was right by his side since they left Minneapolis. They had just inhaled a few grams so he ordered more.

"Last of it," Cousin Vinny sighed and prepared to get chewed out. Everyone around him had a job to do and he had failed his.

"Last of what? Not the coke? I know you ain't telling me, that's the last of the coke!" he boomed. The group of regular groupies knew what to expect and what was expected of them. Pretty Boy was about to clown his cousin and they were required to laugh. They all liked Cousin Vinny but they were about to laugh their asses off at him on cue.

"Already called the homies in O Block. All I gotta do is fall through," Vinny offered like a sacrifice. He was the sacrifice though.

"Cuz you had one job," Pretty Boy began slowly like

when you first turn the fire on under a pot. He liked to include everyone in his roast so it began. "Latanji, what's your job?"

"I suck yo dick!" Latanji shot back. She was actually recruited since she had the best head game in their hometown of Tuscan. She specialized in sucking dick from the back but could suck it from the side just as well. Wasn't much she could do with the limp dick the rapper toted around since he would rather snort and lately smoke coke.

"Lavonda, Michelle..." he went around the jet and asked. They all laid out the duties that got them into the inner circle of groupies. Even if it was a little redundant since every one with a vagina performed a sex act. Except Zenobia but they mutually benefited from the media speculation of whether or not they were dating. Her stock rose by the day and he kept good coke. A fair exchange is no robbery. "You may as well switch up with one of these hoes. You can suck dick and one a 'dem can get the drugs!"

"Naw," Cousin Vinny sighed and just took the abuse in stride. He actually did a lot more than just get drugs. The label paid him a six future salary to keep his cousin out of trouble. That meant getting the drugs so he wouldn't get robbed or arrested, again.

Pretty Boy was a hell of an entertainer but he was dumber than a box of rocks. He thought the label calling him the next R Kelly was a compliment. It wasn't, they just planned to take advantage of him just like they did Robert Kelly. Vinny had peeped the lopsided contracts and hidden faucets designed to leak the mans money into their coffers.

He didn't blow up the spot though in favor of getting cut in on the larceny. That's how he had more money in his personal account than the rapper did in his.

Pretty Boy didn't have a particular penchant for prepubescent pussy like the Pied Piper. Not that he wouldn't pee on a bitch but, his drug of choice was drugs. Any drugs but especially coke. Not just coke, but crack when he could get away with it.

The abuse didn't stop when they landed. He kept riding him all the way over to the hotel and up to the penthouse. The key fob to a brand new Rolls Royce awaited on the table. It was yet another perk of being the rappers do-boy. He drove some of the most expensive cars on the planet without spending a dime.

"I'll run over to the projects and cop that..." Vinny said and moved in to scoop the fob.

"I'll go my damn self. Lavonda, show him how to pop a pussy and y'all can switch jobs!" he laughed as he left.

"I'm finna check in with my girls," Zenobia said since her crew flew commercial. She hadn't spoken to them since the show the night before so she really did need to check in.

"Take a ride with me," he suggested and checking in went out the window.

"OK!" she quickly agreed and shot a group text instead. 'Just landed. See y'all in a minute'

"Mmhm," both Penny and Callie hummed and twisted their lips at the text. Neither replied. They knew she was safe from following her post. She partied hard but hardly wore the brands that she got paid to post.

"This bitch is sweet!" Pretty Boy declared when the double R flashed it's lights in response to the fob.

"Facts!" Zenobia agreed. She knew he didn't know chivalry from a chickens so she opened her own door.

He didn't know O block from any other blocks either so he just went to the first hood he could find. The nearly half a million car turned heads wherever it went but especially in the hood. Prostitutes waved and danced when they saw it. Some actually chased it for blocks until it got away. Which wasn't easy since some of those junkies were pretty quick.

Rats and cats followed along just like the jackers on foot and bikes. The luxury vehicle looked like something to eat and the hood was hungry. All of the youngins on each corner had a pockets full of of crack rocks and pistol full of slugs. Any corner would have done so he pulled over and hopped out.

"Um..." Zenobia tried to warn since she was hood enough to know a wolf in thugs clothing when she saw one. She saw plenty since they flocked to the rich man, dripping drilling with platinum and diamonds.

"Y'all got coke? And crack?" Pretty Boy asked and pulled out a thick roll of cash. The corner boys looked at him, the money, the jewels, then each other. Like if they were trying to see if this was for real. Then they looked around for the hidden cameras to see if they were being pranked. Pretty Boy wagged the cash again and repeated, "Coke, crack?"

"This nigga really is slow!" Zenobia laughed at the comical scene outside the window. She quickly went live to capture the action.

The corner exploded in an instant. One kid grabbed the cash but he was quickly grabbed by two other youths. They fought over the cash while others went for the jewels. Pretty Boy tried to fight but only had two hands. He did have a gun in his back and went for it.

"Back up!" Pretty Boy demanded and waved the gun. It got snatched as soon as he pulled it out.

The teen who grabbed the gun quickly pumped a couple bullets into his torso. The robbers dragged him a few feet trying to snatch the thick chains from his next. One kid braced his foot against Pretty Boy's head to pull the chain off. Two different robbers ran off with one each of his customs Jordan's. They were going to have to work together to them sold.

The youths worked with the ferocity of a pack of piranha and stripped him down to his boxers and wife beater. There was only one thing left to take so the kid with the gun stepped back up and fired a bullet into his brain. He turned and saw a shocked Zenobia holding the camera. A million viewers saw when he raised the gun again and fired. It was pointed directed at the camera when it flashed and everything went dark.

The End, for now....

www.ingramcontent.com/pod-product-compliance
Lightning Source LLC
Chambersburg PA
CBHW051953220626
47052CB00004B/926

* 9 7 8 1 9 5 2 5 4 1 4 5 2 *